RED BURGUNDY

Joan Z. Shore

2012 GG/F
Paris, France

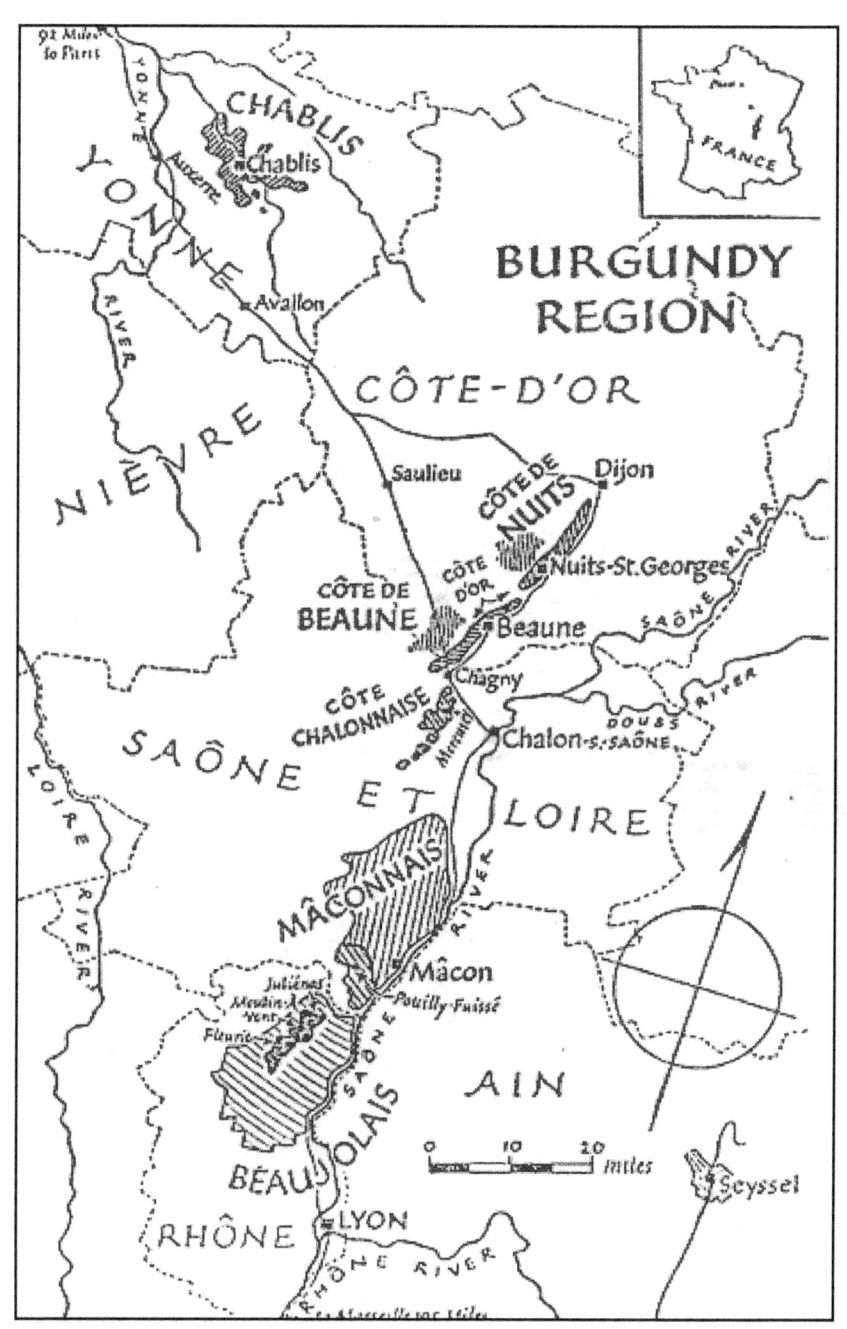

1986

CONTENTS

CHAPTER ONE — *Les Amuse-gueules*

The taxi pulled up to the Gare de Lyon, jerked to a halt and expired like all Citroëns on its cushion of air: pssht.

"Damnedest thing," said George Perkins. "Just can't get used to it."

Helen Perkins, adjusting a sun visor on her short gray hair, was oblivious to automotive suspension.

"Hurry, dear," she said. "We've just got ten minutes to make our train."

George held out a handful of change, all francs and shillings, and looked perplexed. "Hey, can you figure this out? The meter says 32.50."

Helen plucked three ten-franc coins, a five, and a couple of ones from his hand, gave them to the driver, and said, "And our bags, please."

The driver, a young Algerian clad in tight jeans, jumped out, opened the trunk, and heaved the three matched pieces of luggage onto the pavement. He was in no mood to help further, and he jumped back behind the wheel and screeched off.

"Great service," drawled George. "He ought to come to Texas some day and take lessons."

"Hurry," said Helen. "I'll take the two-suiter. Can you manage the big ones?"

They trudged off, as they had been trudging for the past two weeks through London, Amsterdam, Rome and Brussels. Now, after just two days in Paris, they were trudging again to a little town in Burgundy where for one week they would be immersed in French cuisine and fine wines. Pampered. Sheltered. A cooking school in a château, whose manager was British and whose French chef spoke English. Helen sighed with pleasure. It would almost be home.

The train station right now was their last battle, pushing through the crowd, finding the right track, checking with the conductor on the platform (*Oui, c'est le train pour Dijon*), and finding their seats in Compartment 32. Helen held open the heavy glass door, and George dragged in the three bags. He looked despairingly at the overhead rack, then at the suitcases, then at the heavy-set man who was reading *Libération*. The man looked up, realized these were a couple of *touristes*, and rose wheezingly.

Attendez, Monsieur. Je vous donne un coup de main. He took the two-suiter and hoisted it overhead. Then George, feeling embarrassed, helped him hoist up the smaller suitcase. *Et celui-là*, said the Frenchman, *peut rester ici si personne d'autre n'arrive.*

George and Helen understood nothing, but it seemed clear enough that the third suitcase could occupy part of the seat, at least until another passenger came along.

"*Merci,*" said Helen.

They sat down, unbuttoned their raincoats, and smiled weakly at each other. The Frenchman returned to *Libé*. The whistle blew. There was a slight jolt. They were off.

*   *   *

The Nice airport swarmed with the weekend crowd from Paris – the beautiful and less-beautiful people who had left their homes and offices at four-thirty Friday afternoon and were now returning on the six o'clock Sunday evening flight. They had spent every daylight moment lying bare-chested under the shrinking September sun, trying to prolong the suntans they had so carefully cultivated in August.

Stuart Cole and Patti Olsen, from Malibu Beach, were tanner than the others. They also seemed less tired, in spite of three late nights at the gaming tables.

"I really could have used another day here, you know," Stuart said, lurching in front of Patti, lugging a black nylon suitcase with one arm and cradling *The Wall Street Journal* and *The Financial Times* with the other. "I'm sure I could have recouped the rest tonight. And then some."

"Oh, you were lucky to win back what you did," Patti answered. "God, I really freaked out when we were behind three thou."

"Look, you've got to be prepared to lose your shirt. Only I hate to," Stuart said, stopping short in front of the ticket counter marked *'Dijon'*. He fumbled in the pockets of his Armani sports jacket, found the tickets, and plunked them down. He helped Patti lift her two heavy bags off the cart and onto the weighing belt. She kept her make-up case.

"To Dijon?," asked the attendant.

"Yes," said Stuart. "Is it on time?"

Une vingtaine de minutes en retard, she answered. Then, seeing his brow wrinkle in incomprehension, she corrected herself. "About twenty minutes late."

"Shit," he muttered. "I hope they wait for us."

"Pardon?," asked the attendant.

"No, nothing. It's just that we're being picked up at Dijon. With some other people."

The woman shrugged, returned the remainder of the tickets, and set the belt in motion. Arrival at the other end was clearly not her concern.

"Gate five," she said. In English. Patti and Stuart wandered through the crowd, circumvented two scrappy poodles, and stopped briefly at a duty-free toiletries counter.

"Got to get some more Eau Sauvage," he said. "Need anything?"

"Hmmm, yes – some nail polish remover," Patti said. "Though I don't suppose I save much buying it here."

"Doesn't cost much to begin with," Stuart said impatiently. Dammit, he thought, she's got an adding machine in her head. An itty-bitty adding machine in her itty-bitty head.

Patti caught the impatience in his voice. She watched him pick out some after-shave, finger some silk ascots, choose one, and then deftly hand the saleswoman the exact dollar equivalent, converted from Saturday's franc rate. He's got a calculator in his head, she thought, with rue and admiration. And a goddam computer where the heart should be.

Their flight was called. They ran for it.

*   *   *

For nearly two kilometers the road was hemmed with a perfect row of trees on either side, like the pillars of an early Gothic church, arching over the traffic. The big blue

Renault was moving slowly, trailing a sputtering tractor. Richard Silver, behind the wheel, and Barbara, beside him, didn't mind the pace.

"This road is so typical," Barbara said. "I'm sure I've seen it in a hundred French films."

"Uh huh," Richard said, slipping on his sunglasses. The morning sunshine flickered through the row of trees, reminding him of the venetian blinds in his Park Avenue office. He wondered if Alan, his young associate, was managing all right: whether the two prostate jobs went okay, whether the D&C on Diane Schuster...

"You're drifting again," said Barbara. "You're thinking about the office." She had an uncanny way of reading his mind, just by watching his expression. He grinned sheepishly.

"You're right," he said. "Sorry."

"I wish you could leave it all behind you, the way I do," Barbara said.

"It's easy to leave your clients' draperies and wallpaper," Richard said with a light sigh. "It's a lot harder leaving prostates and ovaries."

"Just takes a little practice," Barbara laughed. "Get tough. Pretend they're only curtain hooks and doorknobs!"

Richard squeezed her hand. "I'm glad we got to Mont Saint-Michel," he said. "But Jesus, what a crowd."

"And the travel agent said there wouldn't be many people at this time of the year! What a laugh. But at least he was right about Mère Poulard. Those were great omelettes."

Richard nodded his head, and decided to pull ahead of the tractor. He edged out to the left, then spun the car back into the lane to avoid an oncoming truck.

"Jesus, you can't see what's coming up on these two-lane roads," he said, shaken.

"Oh, take it easy, hon," Barbara said. "We want to stop at the town up ahead anyway, and pick up some stuff for lunch."

"You really think we can pull off the road and picnic? You're sure there isn't some law against it?"

"The Hechts did it last summer," Barbara answered. "And you always see them doing it in French films."

"Old ones," Richard reminded her. "And they're French. They can get away with it."

"Well, we're American, and we pulled them out of two wars and we deserve a little consideration." She smiled at him, checked the guidebook on her lap, and figured out it was about 400 kilometers to Dijon, and 30 more to the château in Lacelle. They would be there just in time for the welcoming *apéritif*.

*   *   *

The early September sun bathed the vineyards in a wash of gold. It had been a warm summer, coming after a chilly spring that nearly nipped the budding vines. It had been a dry summer, too, with just enough rain to plump the grapes so that now, as the last crucial weeks approached, they looked like green marbles. More sun and just enough rain would gradually turn them luscious and purple; too much rain might make them rot, or bloat them and reduce the alcohol content; too little rain would make them dry and shriveled; a flash frost one morning or a five-minute hailstorm would kill them off entirely.

"I tell you, Antoine, it's an act of faith." Lucien Dupuis then set down his *ballon* of *rouge* on the small café table and gazed past his friend at the gentle Burgundian hillside. "Year after year, to tend these vines, to break your back over them as if they're your children, and then have them disappoint you; to watch them take a bad turn or run into some bad luck. And you're helpless. And you wait and hope the next year will be better. It's easier to play the National Lottery." He sighed, and took another draught from the wineglass.

Antoine Didier, a husky man of sixty, looked at his old friend and nodded.

"I know," he said. "I could count on the fingers of one hand the great years, and on the fingers of the other hand the very good years. And the rest..." He shrugged. Then he brightened up. "But I guarantee you, Lucien, this year is going to be very, very good. Maybe a *grand cru*. Like '78. The grapes are fat and hard. They just need four more weeks of this weather. I'm hiring my pickers now, those kids from Paris who are looking for work. I promised them five more francs an hour this year, and said I wouldn't separate the *garçons* and the *filles*. Mixed facilities this year."

"Maybe they'll stay off the streets, then," Lucien huffed. "You remember that brawl last year, right here, when two of your guys flirted with my Brigitte and insulted her fiancé?"

Allez, laughed Antoine. "Your daughter was flattered. Her great misfortune is having a father who's a police inspector. You have no sense of humor."

"Not when it's my daughter," retorted Lucien, "or my sister or my wife."

Antoine smiled quietly. His own wife had died many years ago. He had no daughters, but an only son who had been training in *haute cuisine* since he was eighteen years old: with Troisgros in Roanne, with Vergé in Mougins, with Bocuse in Lyon, and with his own uncle, Gérard Bordet, in Paris. Now, at 27, Vincent Didier was straining to launch his own career, eager to pick up where his uncle Gérard was leaving off, and eager to earn his own three stars.

"Speaking of kids, how is Vincent?," asked Lucien.

"He's well," said Antoine. "He just arrived yesterday to help Gérard with the last class."

"They've gone well this year, those cooking courses?"

"*Formidable. Un grand succès.* Gérard has to turn people away. Vincent says he should take more than ten at a time, but Gérard, you know, he's very serious. He says a crowded kitchen curdles the sauce."

Lucien guffawed. "As a crowded bedroom curdles your passion!"

Laughing, the two men clinked their glasses. A tourist bus rumbled past, raising dust in its wake. It slowed down at the corner, probably so the guide could point out the big war memorial – a monument in the heroic *pompier* style, like so many others in innumerable French towns – with a towering cross, a weeping woman, and a dead soldier. The soldier was wearing a World War One uniform, and the list of names at the base was under the heading 1914-1918. But a second slab had been erected, 1940-1944, and many more names were carved on that.

The bus roared on.

"Americans, probably," remarked Lucien. "After the Côte d'Azur and the Loire Valley, now they're discovering Burgundy!"

He was more amused than annoyed, for he nurtured a certain affection for Americans ever since the war. As adolescents, he and Antoine and Gérard had shared the thrills and dangers of the German Occupation, had pedaled their bicycles out to Normandy to buy butter on the black market, had sneaked into Resistance meetings in their parents' living rooms and begged to be given *une mission* – anything – to prove their patriotism and their manhood. They huddled around the wireless to hear De Gaulle's crackling voice from London, and they waited with excitement for the arrival of – *les Américains*. The General and the Yankees seemed altogether remote and awe-inspiring.

Eh. oui, said Antoine. "We've had so many Americans at the château. It's amazing how crazy they are to learn French cooking. And the Japanese! Only the men come, the chefs mainly, with their cameras and their note-pads. They don't say much, but I think they memorize everything."

"After they copy our cars and our computers, they'll take over the world with our cuisine," Lucien grumbled. "When they start planting grapevines, watch out."

Antoine leaned over, patted him on the back, and rose.

"Well, *cher ami*, that's for our children to worry about. Not us." He pulled out twenty francs from his pocket and put it on the table. "My treat this time. And if the harvest is good, I promise you Champagne."

*   *   *

The Château de St.-Cloud was only 150 years old, but it had been in the Bordet family for more than half that time. It had no stone turrets, like a *château-fort*, and no formal gardens, like a *château-royal*, but it was sturdily and handsomely constructed of red brick and gray stone: only two stories high, with two gabled wings. It was set half a mile back from the main road, flanked by symmetrical outbuildings – the *dépendances*. The hunting lodge, the smokehouse, the oil press, and the poultry shed were in a separate, long building on the left; the old stables, the barn, and the caretaker's house – the handsome gate-house, where Antoine lived – were on the right. The wine cave, with its great oak casks and shelf-lined walls of chalk, was farther on, behind the stables.

In back of the château was a small flower garden, a large vegetable garden, and an orchard. A tennis court, built recently, lay just at the boundary of the vineyard.

Ancient chestnut trees spotted the property, and two amiable-looking stone lions marked the entrance to the pebbled courtyard. Topiary trees framed the central arched doorway, which was crowned with a Dutch-style pediment set with a large clock. Somehow, all the elements worked together, and although the château was the most imposing building in Lacelle, and the pride of the villagers, it reflected the comfortable, homey style of the early nineteenth-century *bourgeoisie* rather than the pretentious airs of the later *nouveaux-riches*.

Gérard Bordet had inherited it when he was forty, after his father's death. A bachelor, with a thriving restaurant in Paris, Gérard wondered how he could run the château and its three acres of prime vineyards and also keep his *main à la pâte* at La Boule d'Argent.

C'est impossible, he said. "If I leave La Boule now, I'll never get my third star." Finally, he found the solution: his sister, Marie-Anne, and her husband, Antoine, would manage the estate. They moved in immediately, with their four-year old son, Vincent.

Vincent adored the château; no, he coveted it. As a little boy, he loved inviting his friends *chez moi* and running around the empty rooms in the wings. They chased the chickens in the *poulailler,* cranked the heavy stone oil press, and had a *goûter* – an afternoon snack – in the big pantry. Later, in high school, he organized parties – *boums,* they were called – in the barn. He forgot then that he was only the owner's nephew, and that his father was only the manager. In back of his head, even at sixteen, he knew someday he would inherit St.-Cloud.

Gérard had a mild heart attack just before he turned sixty. His doctor advised him to let up.

"Sois sage, mon vieux. You've had too much of your own good cooking, too much St.-Cloud Burgundy, too much stress at work." He used the English word "stress" because it was becoming fashionable. Executives suffered from *le stress*; so did politicians; so why not a three-star chef?

Gérard scowled. "You want to put me out to pasture already? Brillat-Savarin lived past seventy. Escoffier lived to nearly ninety. How many chefs do you know who die young?"

But reason prevailed, to a degree. Grudgingly, Gérard turned over the daily pre-dawn shopping at Rungis to his assistant. He stopped working on Sundays. He closed La Boule d'Argent for two months during the summer instead of one. And then, Sybil Dickson, a British food critic, asked him why he didn't run summer cooking classes at the château.

Why not?, thought Gérard. Then he thought of all the problems: converting the enormous old kitchen into a professional facility, repairing and remodeling the wings to make comfortable guest rooms, sprucing up the shabby salon...

But in the end, he did it, mainly with Sybil's help and encouragement. She wrote a brochure for him, sent out press releases, and spread the word among her colleagues. The first summer was hard, with very few applicants. Sybil arranged special visits for the press, but everything that could have gone wrong went wrong. The weather was rainy and cold – a disaster for the vines and a discouragement for visitors. The new electric range was poorly installed and needed continual repairs. The new roof on the east wing started to spring leaks, which stained the fresh wallpaper. Shipments of seafood from Brittany got delayed because of a truckers' strike.

"We're *en rodage*," Sybil chirped cheerfully, with her funny British accent. "Just breaking in. Don't worry, Gérard.

Next year will be marvelous."

And it was. Applications began pouring in as early as February. Several travel agents organized special stopovers as part of their regular Burgundy tours. Even the French press began to speak of "Bordet's baby" – *La Boule Qui Roule en Bourgogne*. Gérard appointed Sybil his business manager, and she spent most of the summer at St.-Cloud, joined once during each season, for two weeks, by her American husband.

This summer, the third, had surpassed their expectations. A Japanese hotel chain, hearing about the courses, sent several groups of chefs to do a week-long apprenticeship. Some Swiss and German *restaurateurs* dropped in to inspect the program and see if they could adapt it back home, in a châlet or *Schloss*. But the bulk of the guests, and the most avid students, were Americans. They came with relish and reverence. They insisted on chopping, stirring, beating and tasting everything, and they had enormous appetites.

"It's not *la grande bouffe* here," Gérard would admonish them. "It's *la bonne bouffe*."

* * *

Sybil kept the prettiest room for herself. It was at the end of the west wing, past three guest rooms, with an adjoining private bath. The walls were covered in rose *toile de Jouy*. An old Aubusson carpet covered part of the gleaming parquet floor, and the furniture – scavenged out by Sybil herself in local shops – was real French Provincial.

She had an *ébéniste* in town check all the hinges and replace missing plugs. ("*Never*, Monsieur, must you use a nail," she had fairly shrieked at the poor man, seeing him one day with a mouthful of tacks.) She had the maid, Colette, polish the armoire and bureau at least once a month, with Goddard's furniture wax. And every spring, before her arrival, the matching *toile* draperies and sheer *voilettes* were taken down, carefully washed, and rehung.

"Of course, the pollution here isn't anything like New York," she admitted, "but a thorough cleaning once a year is the absolute minimum."

She welcomed the summers in Burgundy, for her life in New York was hectic. She still was writing a regular column for a British newspaper, and she often was called upon as a food consultant or lecturer. (Mainly at ladies' luncheons, she lamented.) Her husband, Daniel, was a successful partner in a successful firm that arranged successful mergers. Nothing lamentable about that, really, for success allowed them to have a Fifth Avenue apartment, send their two sons to boarding school, and maintain a small summer home in the Hamptons. She realized that the job at St.-Cloud was taking up more and more of her time, but in many ways it was the icing on the cake: it meant at least two trips to France every year, including the long summer holiday, when New York was too hot and the Hamptons too crowded.

Best of all, Sybil truly liked working with Gérard. She had been going to his Parisian restaurant for years, and had often written it up – so often and so glowingly, in fact, that her editor once asked her pointedly if she were having an affair with the *propriétaire*. Gérard always had a new creation for her to sample, and she always regaled him with catty stories of new Manhattan restaurants that opened with fanfare, flew high for a while, and failed.

"Even with a French-trained chef," she confided, wide eyed, "they can't make it in New York."

"Why?," Gérard asked, over and over.

"Because they've got frozen products and fickle clients and fantastic overhead." Sybil knew the answer by heart.

She was shocked when she heard about Gérard's heart attack, and called him while he was still in the hospital.

Mon cher ami, she said with her funny French accent. "I always warned you about cholesterol."

Ecoute, Sybil, Gérard answered weakly, *c'est juste une petite crise. Rien de grave.*

"Nothing grave?," Sybil cried, not bothering to translate. "The only thing more serious than the first heart attack is the last one. Gérard, you've got to take this as a warning. You've got to let up." Surprisingly, she began to sob.

"That's what my doctor says. *C'est le stress*. He says it's not in my body, it's in my head."

"It's in your body now, too. What are you going to do about it?"

They talked for a long time, like two old schoolmates, and Sybil finally said, "Gérard, why don't you take the summer off and just run some cooking classes at the château?"

And so he did.

Gradually, the cooking school took on a life of its own.

Gérard loved showing off to the students: how quickly he boned a fish, how deftly he rolled a *mille-feuille*. They watched him with fascination, as he had raptly watched his own teacher, forty years ago, as a young apprentice. He was, after all, a born showman, and he realized how isolated he had been all these years, in the kitchen of La Boule d'Argent, only emerging once or twice during the evening to make a polite round of the tables. And even that he avoided when his *maître d'hôtel* told him a particularly fawning food critic was in the dining room.

Merde!, Gérard would mutter. "He's here for another free dinner."

Sybil never fawned, and often she surprised Gérard with really clever ideas. Like suggesting he use mango with the *magret de canard* instead of kiwis. ("Kiwis are so dreadfully overdone," she insisted, "and so utterly bland.") Or putting mint in his chocolate mousse instead of orange, and serving it with a *crème de menthe* liqueur.

Once, late at night at the château, when they had been poring over the ledger for hours, she whipped up an *omelette aux lardons* for them to share, and he was astonished by her expertise.

"You ought to take over the classes one day," he said, "after I'm gone."

She laughed. "And have your ghost howl at me for every *faux pas* I make? No, thank you."

Sérieusement, he said, "you're very good. You have the knack."

"But my dear Gérard, I don't have the patience. I would

simply go out of my mind playing teacher." She sipped her Saint-Véran thoughtfully. "In fact, to tell you the truth, I sometimes wonder if Vincent is going to enjoy teaching here. The boy is so tense and high-strung."

"He gets that from his grandfather. *Papa* was a tyrant. He knew he had the best piece of land in the region – the best soil, the best drainage, the best slope for the sun. *Mon dieu!*, he lorded it over everyone. The only thing bigger than his arrogance was his waistline."

"Well, Vincent isn't arrogant yet," mused Sybil, "but I don't think it will be long before he is. He makes such nasty remarks about the other growers. He doesn't realize that all these families are struggling, each one with its own little plot. Instead, he acts like a rich wine baron from Bordeaux, with enormous acreage and a family fortune."

"It's true," agreed Gerard. "He will have to learn a little humility, and try harder to get along with the neighbors. We are so divided already."

They sat quietly for a while. Then Gérard brightened up.

"But he's good in the kitchen, my Vincent. Don't you think so?"

"Yes, he is," Sybil admitted. But there again, she had reservations. Vincent seemed to attack the food, rather than prepare it. He had a fearsome physical approach, while all the great chefs she had met were intellectual, even sensual, toward their ingredients. To them, cooking was like an act of love.

"Vincent needs to be softer," she said. "He's lacking love."

"Ah, love," said Gérard. "Give him time. The boy is still young. He hasn't met anyone yet."

"No, I mean love for the métier," explained Sybil. "He's always in such a hurry to get done, he doesn't seem to enjoy the process of getting there. I sometimes imagine him turning the Château de St.-Cloud into a MacDonald's."

Gérard laughed. "Well, that may be what his generation is coming to."

He collected the plates and put them in the sink for Colette to wash in the morning. Sybil wiped the omelette pan with paper toweling and hung it back up on the pantry wall. It was past one o'clock. They were both yawning.

"Gérard," Sybil said as they slowly walked upstairs to their rooms, "speaking of love, why didn't you ever get married?"

"Ah," smiled Gérard, "because I never found anyone."

Sybil looked at him quizzically.

"You never found anyone?"

"Anyone who could cook as well as I."

*　　*　　*

Sunday in Lacelle was the quietest day of the week. The church bells rang in the morning to announce the two masses, then were silent until evening vespers. The *boulangerie*, the only shop to open, closed promptly at noon. A few men, young bachelors and elderly widowers, hung around the café in mid-afternoon discussing the state of the grapes and the bad deal they were getting from the

Common Market. (*"C'est incroyable!* Up in Brussels, those technocrats don't give a damn about us."*)

That Sunday, at the Château de St.-Cloud, Sybil was handing out orders like a general mounting the last campaign. It was, indeed, the last course of the summer; by next Saturday at lunchtime the diplomas would be given out. The guests would finish their packing and be driven to the train station. Daniel, who had spent the last week at the château, would leave with them, to return to New York. Sybil would stay on one week longer to settle all the accounts with Gérard. Then they would drive up to Paris in his battered Peugeot, talking about how the summer went but mostly thinking about the *rentrée*. Gérard would be planning his menus for the coming season, and considering staff changes. Sybil would be making mental lists of things she had to do in New York: sending the boys off to school, catching up on the local news, and outlining some story ideas for her paper. Perhaps it was just sentimental, like the song, but she always looked forward to autumn in New York.

Colette burst into the salon with a can of furniture wax.

"Oh, no," said Sybil, addressing her in French. "There are more important things right now. The silver coffee service needs to be polished and the floor needs to be swept. And have you checked the towels in the bathrooms?"

She was pleased how much her French had improved these past three summers, although Gérard still made fun of her accent.

"And you," she countered, "you speak English like

a *vache espagnole*." It was an expression she had learned in French class at school, and although she never understood the connection between a Spanish cow and doing something badly, she knew it was a nice, old-fashioned insult that could be used in the best of company.

From Vincent, on the other hand, she learned the phrase *vachement bien*, which for some obscure reason meant "awfully good". Why, she wondered, do the French always pick on the poor old cow?

She glanced at her watch: two-thirty. They should be starting to arrive. The train from Paris at three-twenty, the plane from Nice at four, and the couple driving from Brittany – if they didn't lose their way – any time up to five. Antoine would drive to the train station in Dijon to get the Perkins' and the two Japanese guests; Vincent would go to the airport to pick up the couple from California. The remaining two guests were still a mystery: a certain Count Stefano di Carozza who was driving up sometime from Milan, and a friend of his named Lucinda Contini who was arriving later in the week from Geneva. A nice smorgasbrod of nationalities, she thought. As usual.

She went into the small office and began making photocopies of the menus and recipes for the first day. The menus changed gradually over the course of the summer, reflecting the weekly changes in the market, but the class structure never varied: the preparation of an *entrée*, a *plat principal*, and a dessert every morning followed by lunch, which consisted of those three courses; then two hours off for napping, strolling, or tennis; and a demonstration class in the afternoon, which usually involved something very complicated or traditional, which was then served for dinner.

During the week, several excursions were planned to local vintners and to a typical Burgundian two-star restaurant. At least one afternoon was devoted to a walk through the St.-Cloud vineyard and a visit to the wine cellar. That was where Antoine took over, masterfully explaining the whole process, from the *pied* in the ground to the cork in the bottle. Then he held a tasting of various St.-Cloud vintages compared with other regional labels. He was fair, but the St.-Cloud always got top honors. It was a truly exceptional Burgundy, and the guests who couldn't actually taste and appreciate the difference were surely impressed by the fact that they were present at the source. Nearly everyone bought a case to take home.

Sybil scooped up the pile of photocopies and placed them on the stack of aprons and hand-towels that she would distribute tomorrow. She went into the pantry and took down a silver tray and thirteen wine glasses. Mentally, she checked again: eight guests, Gérard, Antoine and Vincent, Daniel and myself. She smiled. Antoine would make a fuss about having thirteen at the table tonight, and probably go off and sit with Vincent to avoid bad luck. Now, how do you explain that particular French psychosis to a band of foreigners?

She opened a fresh bottle of *crème de cassis* and looked in the fridge to make sure the white Sauvignon was well chilled. She always served *kir* for the welcoming *apéritif*, and always told the story about its invention: how, many years ago, Canon Kir of Dijon, a clever churchman, got the bright idea of salvaging poor quality white wine by pouring a little *cassis* into it and serving the blend as a cocktail. Sybil considered that just another indication of French genius – and guile: the kind of mentality that creates fashion and perfume and bloated goose livers.

Daniel walked in, waving his tennis racket.

"Hi, love. I'm off for a few sets with Vincent."

"Alright, dear, but please get back in time to change and give me a hand." Sybil hardly looked up. "And please be careful not to track in anything on the carpet."

It always amazed her how a man like Daniel, born in Boston and a proud product of proper Eastern schools, could be so careless around the house. He had the same nonchalance whether they were at home in Manhattan, visiting his parents at Nantucket, or here at the château. The only place where he seemed strict and immaculate was at his office, a seven-room suite on Wall Street, where every Barcelona chair was immovably positioned and every ashtray had an eternal resting place.

Once she asked him why. "Why aren't you a little like that at home?"

"The beauty of it is I don't have to be like that at home," he grinned. "Business is business and home is home."

And never the twain shall meet, Sybil thought, with a silent moan. Daniel's life was compartmentalized like that. They took business associates to certain restaurants and went with friends to others. They had a silver-gray BMW for evening use and a Volvo for jaunts to the Hamptons. Daniel smoked seven-dollar Davidoffs in the office and Marlboros at home. Once, after a bitter argument between them, Sybil wondered whether he didn't have a counterpart to her: an upscale mistress at Sutton Place, for example.

But their arguments were rare. They lived compatible, parallel lives, each one amused – and bemused – by what the other was doing. She sometimes felt it was a funny twist of fate, that after fighting so hard with her parents to go to an American college and getting accepted to Wellesley, she would then meet Daniel at the end of her sophomore year and never return to England – and never finish college. For that year Daniel was graduating from law school and taking a job in New York, so it was a question of following along or losing him forever. Or so she believed.

Success came quickly to him. After eight years with an investment banking firm, he was asked to join John Talbot and David Levey as an associate in their newly-formed company, specializing in mergers and acquisitions. Five years later, Daniel was made a full partner, and the firm's name was changed to Talbot, Levey and Dickson.

"Here's to TLD – Tender Loving Dementia," Sybil giggled, as they celebrated the news with Champagne and *foie gras* at La Côte Basque.

Tender and loving it wasn't; demented it was. Daniel usually worked until seven-thirty at night, and spent at least two Saturdays a month doing catch-up work at the office. Increasingly, there was overseas travel, and once the boys were away at school, Sybil prevailed upon him to go along, especially on the trips to London and Paris. On one of those trips, she met an old school chum who was writing on fashion for *The Observer*. She told Sybil she should write a lifestyle column from New York. But the editor-in-chief said he hated the word "lifestyle" even more than the concept of lifestyle, and suggested she do a straight food column instead.

"The Americans advising the English on food?," a French colleague of Daniel's asked incredulously. "That's rather what we call *un dialogue de sourds* – a dialogue between the deaf."

"Well, it's not advice exactly," Sybil tried to explain, even as she tried to dispel the preposterous notion in her own mind. "It's going to be more like a report or survey. Restaurant reviews, and things like that."

And so her career began. It didn't take too much time away from home, it didn't interfere with Daniel's schedule, and it earned her a little money that she quietly squirreled away. She used her press credentials to get invited to culinary events, and, best of all, to get prompt and polite service at the top restaurants. A little note to Taillevent on her personal stationery assured her of a table on two weeks' notice. Her New York friends envied her.

"My God, we've been trying for years to get in there," said her upstairs neighbor. "They say we have to write six months in advance."

Overall, thought Sybil, I've been very lucky. My life has fallen into place in a nice, neat way. No tragedies, no earth shaking upheavals, no sweaty sleepless nights. She tapped the wooden saltbox with her knuckles.

"*Que ça dure.*" May it last.

* * *

Helen and George Perkins were the first ones downstairs. Accustomed by now to packing and unpacking every few days, they made quick work of it. Helen's dacron knits were hung in the armoire, and George simply suspended his two-suiter on the door-hook. Helen was charmed by the small, cheerful room.

"It's real French style!" she marveled.

George was moderately relieved to find a shower extension hanging over the bathroom tub.

"I guess the French haven't discovered stall showers yet," he mumbled.

Sybil greeted them at the foot of the stairs, and introduced Daniel.

"Let's just wait a few minutes for the others to come down, and I'll show you all around. Oh, here comes Mr. Okura and Mr. Takashi. You didn't meet each other on the train, did you? No, I figured you would probably be in different compartments."

The two Japanese gentlemen, Nikons around their necks, murmured something and bowed. George, his hand outstretched and untaken, fumbled for a moment and then nodded his head. Sybil led them out the front door onto the graveled courtyard.

"The château has been in the Bordet family since 1890," she started to explain. "Before that, it belonged to Charles de la Tour, who inherited it from his father, Henri."

The Japanese were busily snapping pictures, but the Perkins seemed to be listening, albeit listlessly, so she chatted on.

"Henri de la Tour was a lieutenant in Napoleon's army. He was seriously injured in the battle of Leipzig so he was retired, and with his pension, plus some family money, he built this château. Then he replanted the vineyard, which had been untended for many years, and it turned out to be one of the best vineyards in the entire Burgundy region."

George wanted to know how many bottles were produced every year, and how much the wine cost in France and what the mark-up was in the U.S. Sybil, her train of thought broken, started to answer but then the Silvers came out the door. Sybil introduced them to the others.

"I'm so glad you had a good drive over from Brittany," she said to Richard. "I was afraid you'd have some trouble. These secondary roads are so confusing."

"Compared to Paris, it was easy," Barbara laughed. "The rental agent brought the car over to our hotel, and then left us. I thought we'd never get past the Place de l'Etoile."

"I wouldn't drive in Paris if you paid me," said George. "Our taxi diver nearly hit three cars on the way to the train station."

"Oh, you get used to it," said Daniel. "Next to tax evasion, it's the favorite French pastime."

Barbara cast him an admiring smile. He seemed cool and knowledgeable. He smiled back.

Sybil glanced at her watch. "Let me go see if the other two guests are ready. We really ought to be starting."

She hurried back inside, went upstairs, and was about to knock on the door when she heard a commotion. Ms. Olsen was shrieking. Mr. Cole apparently was trying to calm her. Sybil couldn't make any sense of it and decided to go ahead and knock. The shrieking continued. She knocked again. This time it was heard. The shrieking stopped and the door opened. It was Stuart.

"Oh, I'm sorry," he said. "We've had a little problem. I mean, Patti's had a little problem. She burned her ear with her electric curling iron."

Sybil looked at Patti. The young woman was hanging over the bed, her hands cupping her right ear, her blond hair straggling over her face. She was sobbing.

"Oh dear," said Sybil. "Let me get you some ointment."

She went to her room, and returned quickly with a tube of *onguent pour brûlures.*

"I always keep it handy in case there are accidents in the kitchen," she explained. "Here, let me help you."

Patti took a deep breath and stood up. She brushed her hair to one side and gratefully let Sybil apply the cream to the reddened rim of her ear.

"Rather nasty," said Sybil. "Here, keep the whole tube until tomorrow. You can reapply it every few hours."

"Thank you," Patti sniffed.

"Everyone's downstairs, waiting for my little tour of the property. Do you feel up to it?"

Patti didn't think so.

"You go, Stu," she said. "I'll just rest a bit."

Stuart looked at her, with more annoyance than concern, thought Sybil, and said okay, he'd go.

"Really sorry about that," he said to Sybil as they went downstairs. "I told her we were late, but she insisted on touching up her hair."

Sybil said it was perfectly alright; she was probably tired from the trip anyway. She'd get to see the grounds another time.

A new person had joined the group in the courtyard – a tall, distinguished-looking man who was leaning against a red Ferrari, which was obviously his and which was being admired by everyone, including the Japanese. Sybil walked briskly over, sensing that this must be Stefano di Carozza.

"Hello," she said. "Are you Count di Carozza?"

"That's right. And you are Mrs. Dickson?" He smiled, taking her hand and raising it halfway to his lips. It was the gesture of a man of "a certain age" (as the French always say about middle-aged women), who had been raised in an upper class family and who had lived long enough to see the demise of hand-kissing. To kiss a woman's hand today would mark one as terribly *vieux jeu*, but not to do it would deprive one of a charming opening. The halfway measure, it seemed, indicated maturity and breeding, while suggesting one was modern and enterprising and willing to go further.

"I'm so glad you managed to get here today," said Sybil, wondering how much further this interesting man would go. He had a strange but delightful accent – northern

Italy? – and he seemed sublimely self-assured. It was not, she thought, the self-assurance of a Harvard graduate: she had seen plenty of that among Daniel's colleagues. Rather, it was the assurance of a man who probably had been born with a silver spoon and had, through cunning and connections, parlayed it into a goldmine.

Everyone had introduced themselves, so Sybil herded them together and started off in the direction of the hunting lodge, the oil press, and the *poulailler*. Di Carozza stayed close to her – too close, she thought. Had he already staked her out as his prey for the week? What nonsense! He was at the age where he would prefer easier conquests: 25-year old stewardesses and 30-year old secretaries, who would fawn over the Ferrari. Certainly not a 40-year old food writer. Women of forty require hard work and novelty, Sybil reflected complacently. They've heard all the lines and learnt most of the repliques. They're wary and cynical. Only a man of great energy and imagination might, possibly, move them.

She realized she was thinking from the vantage point of a perfectly faithful wife, who had rarely, if ever, entertained ideas of sexual abandon. She also realized she was forgetting her small troupe.

"Now, these outbuildings, the *dépendances*, were the support structure for the entire estate," she said, stopping in front of the hunting lodge. She pointed to a huge hook emerging from the façade near the second floor window. "That's where the game was hung. The gamekeeper lived inside and was in charge of all the curing and smoking."

She led them around to the back of the long building into the *poulailler,* which presented an ordinary barnyard scene of hens scratching, roosters strutting, and ducks waddling.

"Very ordinary," she said, "but very necessary to the life of the château, then and now. We get dozens of eggs every week, and we use the old hens for our *coq au vin.*"

She took them into the storage room. Shelves lined the walls up to the ceiling, most of them laden with jars of preserves and sweet-smelling apples, left over from last year's harvest. Bunches of pungent herbs hung from the ceiling, drying in the cool air.

Next door was the huge stone press – a circular millstone on a round base that had a trough running around it.

"We're not sure about this," said Sybil. "It looks like an olive press, but there are no olive trees in the region. We think perhaps the original owners had olives shipped up from Provence and pressed their own oil here."

She was startled as a series of flashes went off; the two Japanese guests were taking pictures. She caught Daniel's eye and grinned at him. He grinned back and gave a little shrug. They entertained many Japanese businessmen in New York, and had learned never to make fun of their mania. But behind their backs, Daniel called them the Snapanese.

Sybil led the group across the courtyard to the barn and stables, which would be used as sleeping quarters for the grape pickers next month. Thin shafts of sunlight pierced the roof, playing on the beams and the piles of musty hay. George wondered aloud why the roof wasn't tiled in asphalt.

Barbara thought it would make a lovely artist's loft. Stefano, hands in his pockets, seemed divinely bored. The Japanese snapped away.

"And this," Sybil said, standing in front of the small brick gate-house, "is where Antoine lives. He's here year-round, and thanks to him, the St.-Cloud label has the coveted *appellation contrôlée*."

She never talked down to her guests, but always assumed they had at least a modicum of knowledge about French wine and food. Otherwise, why would they be here?

She showed them the well – a pit fifty meters deep that was level with the ground. The stone wall and bucket had been removed many years ago, and the treacherous hole was now covered with a heavy metal plaque. At Sybil's request, Daniel stooped down and pulled it aside, so everyone could peer into the depths.

"During the Occupation," explained Sybil, "local Resistance fighters hid weapons and explosives down here, attached to a pulley. After the German retreat, they threw all the remaining arms into the pit. They're still there."

Daniel pushed the cover back on, and they all walked to the rear of the château. Sybil pointed out the vegetable garden, the fruit trees, and the tennis court. She felt like the *châtelaine* of the property; indeed, in a way she was, being the only woman to live there on a regular basis. Poor Marie-Anne, Antoine's wife, had died long before Sybil ever got involved with St.-Cloud, and according to the townspeople, she had been a frail creature who left the running of the property to her brother and husband. She'd been a sweet, indulgent mother to Vincent, spoiling the boy needlessly, and she had been a devoted, undemanding wife to Antoine. Except during periods of poor health, she went to mass every Sunday, and was forever inviting Père André, the parish priest, back to the château for a copious Sunday lunch.

Gérard sometimes got impatient with her; she was so vague and impractical, so unlike their robust mother, who ran the château with an iron hand and knew where every centime was spent. *Maman* argued constantly with *papa* and rarely lost a fight, being clever enough to make him think her ideas were originally his. But Marie-Anne! – she would quietly remove herself from any argument and go off to read her breviary.

"She's praying her way out of it," Antoine would explain. "And you've got to admit it, God is still on her side."

Finally, though, even God left her, in exasperation. She died of influenza.

Sybil led her group back to the courtyard, glanced at the ornate clock over the portal, and announced it was time for cocktails. She knew the timing was perfect: after a long day of travel and a polite tour of the grounds, everyone was ready to collapse in an armchair. They would be grateful for anything now, she smiled wickedly to herself. Even tap water. Tomorrow it would be different. They would be fresh and rested and clamoring for their money's worth of good food and undivided attention.

Stuart went upstairs to collect Patti. Stefano went upstairs with Vincent to deposit his two Vuitton bags in his room. The others followed Sybil into the salon and did, indeed, sink gratefully into the chairs and sofas. Right on cue, Colette scurried in with the tray of glasses and Antoine followed her with the white wine and *crème de cassis*. George asked if there wasn't possibly some Scotch around; Sybil said yes, there probably was, but wouldn't he like to try some *kir* first? Stefano sauntered into the room, and Sybil told her *kir* story.

"So typical of the French," he said. "If they can't make good things better, they'll make bad things worse."

Sybil glanced at him, annoyed at his arrogance, and decided to parry with him on his own ground.

"The French always say *le mieux est l'ennemi du bien*: What's better is the enemy of what's already good."

"Then it must follow that what's worse is the enemy of what's already bad," Stefano smiled. "And *kir* is certainly an abomination of wine."

"Would you prefer some plain Sauvignon?," Sybil asked, gritting her teeth and raising the bottle.

"No, thank you," said Stefano, still smiling. "I'll stay with the folklore." And he raised his glass, nodding charmingly to Sybil.

What on earth is he doing here?, she wondered. He's certainly not the type to take lessons about anything from anybody, and I'm sure he never steps foot into a kitchen except to fetch ice cubes or pinch the maid. She looked quizzically over to Daniel, but he was talking to the Silvers. Stuart was gazing out the long French window, standing behind Patti who was curled up on an armchair. Her blond hair was combed adroitly over the reddened ear. The Perkins, seated side by side on a sofa, were leafing through a Fielding Guide. The Japanese were trying to communicate with Gérard and Antoine. Straining to hear them, Sybil couldn't decide whose English was worse. How were they ever going to get through the week, these Asians, unless they watched like hawks and scribbled in shorthand?

She realized Colette still hadn't brought in the *amuse-gueules* – the assortment of snacks and hors d'oeuvres to nibble with the drinks. She ran into the kitchen and saw Colette squatting on the floor, gathering up two dozen piping hot cheese puffs. She looked up, startled.

Excusez-moi, Madame, she stammered. "They fell as I took the baking sheet out of the oven."

"Oh, Lord," Sybil mumbled. Too late to do anything now but pick them up and serve them. She bent down next to Colette wondering how many culinary errors gave rise to a great new dish, how many were irretrievable disasters, and how many more were blithely overlooked and eaten. So be it with this one, she sighed.

She arranged them appetizingly on the silver platter, next to the bowl of *champignons* à *la grècque* and *cornichons*, picked up the stack of cocktail napkins, and carried it all triumphantly into the salon. Eyes hungered and mouths watered, and the puffs quickly disappeared.

"That's the bottom line," she told herself with a shrug. "Ignorance is delicious."

*   *   *

CHAPTER TWO – *Les Entrées*

Breakfast was over. It was always a simple meal – coffee and croissants and homemade jam – served in the pantry, where everyone sat on stools at the high counter. Patti had been looking forward to breakfast in bed, just as she had it on the Côte d'Azur, but Stuart was glad to have an excuse to avoid that. He hated the crumbs on the sheets, and invariably, Patti spilled coffee on his pajamas.

Barbara and Richard had already taken a stroll around the château – Richard, in fact, had put on his Adidas and jogged down to the main road and back, then out to the tennis court. Helen and George arrived in the pantry right on time looking a little rumpled and bleary-eyed. Stefano had not been seen at all, and Colette, going upstairs to start the housecleaning, told Sybil his bedroom door was still locked. Sybil shrugged. It was like him.

They filed out of the pantry into the large sunny kitchen. It had whitewashed walls and a high beamed ceiling. On one side, a wide window faced the entrance court, and on the other side, high French doors led out to the herb garden in back. The far wall was hung with bright copper pots and old wrought iron utensils, and a long oak shelf displayed a collection of local pottery.

The work area, running the length of the fourth wall, was a startling anachronism in this setting: polished cabinets of stainless steel, gas and electric burners set into aluminum countertops, a sleek wall oven and oversized refrigerator, slide-away chopping boards and appliances, and a large mirror hanging at an angle overhead to reflect the work surfaces.

"No microwave oven," Patti remarked to Stuart.

"Thank heavens," Barbara responded archly.

Gérard and Sybil arrived with piles of papers, and fresh aprons and towels bearing the school's name and symbol: a casserole on a cloud. It was, of course, a little word-play with the château's name – St.-Cloud – which didn't mean "cloud" at all in French. But Sybil liked the bilingual *double entendre*, and convinced Gérard that the image would have meaning to anyone who spoke English.

"Be sure to wear your aprons when you're working here," she said crisply, handing them out. "And use the towels to handle hot dishes and wipe up spills." Then she passed around the Xeroxed copies of the day's menu: *quenelles de brochette, lapin marchand de vin. salade frisée au crotin chaud,* and *tarte Tartin.*

"Oh God, rabbit," said Barbara. "I'd never serve that in New York."

"I don't know," said Richard. "The kids might get a kick out of it!"

"Gruesome idea," Barbara concluded.

Gérard set out the ingredients for the rabbit. It had to marinate for several hours, he explained, so he would start that first. He took three skinned rabbits from the refrigerator, all quite bloody, with popping eyes. Without their fur, they looked emaciated. But fur remained around their feet, like mittens, and Sybil said that was the French regulation, to prove they were indeed rabbits and not cats – a cheap substitution that some unscrupulous butchers used to foist on their unwitting customers. Barbara looked in horror at Richard. Patti wrinkled her nose. Daniel had heard the story before and said in Sybil's ear, rather too loudly, "meow."

"Hush," she said, and smiled encouragingly at Gérard to continue.

With a huge cleaver, Gérard hacked the rabbits into serving-size pieces. Then he prepared the marinade, pouring a whole bottle of red Burgundy into a large earthenware bowl. Quickly, expertly, he sliced three large onions and six carrots, peeled and crushed six cloves of garlic, and rinsed a handful of fresh parsley and thyme. He threw it all into the bowl, then added the rabbit pieces, and put it aside to marinate.

Sybil provided a running commentary on the procedure, for much as Gérard hated to speak English, he hated it even more while he was working.

"We'll just forget that for two hours," she said cheerfully, as Gérard gathered up the heads, the tails, and the twelve furry feet and threw it all into the waste bin. He kept the livers, however, for they would be used tomorrow in a *pâté*.

Next came the *quenelles*. Gérard took three large, silvery pike, purchased early that morning in the Macon market, and lined them up on the counter. With a fine-bladed knife, he deftly removed their heads and snipped off their tails and fins with scissors. Then, with a finer knife, he opened their bellies and pulled out the guts. With a paring knife, he lifted away the bones.

"You want to try?," he asked Barbara, who was hovering over the counter, fascinated.

"Well, alright," she said, deciding it was probably time she learned to filet a fish. Gingerly, she began scraping away the bones, her fingertips barely touching the slimy flesh.

"Don't be afraid!," roared Gérard. "He's already dead!"

Barbara took a deep breath and a firmer grip. The flesh came off in several pieces, but Sybil assured her it didn't matter, because everything would be pounded and puréed anyway for the *quenelles*. Gérard, meanwhile, prepared the *panada* – the milk and breadcrumb mixture that would be added to the fish. He used three cups of crumbs to every cup of milk, poured it into a mortar, and pounded the mixture until it was completely smooth. Then he returned to the fish, picking out the tiny bones that Barbara had overlooked. He sprinkled the mound of fish with salt, pepper and nutmeg, put it all in another mortar, and pounded that for five minutes. Then he combined the *panada* and the fish, added 500 grams of butter, and pounded some more. When it was well blended, he added six eggs, one at a time, breaking each one with a smart flick of his wrist. Vincent, at the far end of the counter, was also busy with eggs: he was opening and separating a dozen of them. The yolks were handed over to Gérard and the bowl full of whites was put in the refrigerator.

"For tomorrow's meringues," explained Sybil, who saw expressions of bewilderment on many faces, and astonishment, too, at the lavish use of products.

Gérard was adding the yolks, and passing the mortar around for everyone to stir. It seemed an endless process, and when he began the last step – passing the mixture through a sieve – Helen couldn't control herself any longer.

"Can't you use a blender to do all that?," she exclaimed.

"Yes, of course," answered Sybil. "That's mentioned in a footnote on the recipe. But, you see, Gérard is a purist from the old school of cuisine. He believes you have to feel your ingredients at every step of the way."

Helen was shaking her head in disbelief, but she said no more. The idea of spending half an hour doing by hand what a machine could do in three minutes (medium speed setting) just didn't make sense to her.

Imperturbably, Gérard took a wooden spoon and stirred the marinating rabbit. Then, as he started to assemble the *tarte Tatin*, Stefano sauntered in. He nodded to Gérard with a smile, and walked over to Sybil.

Bonjour, chère Madame.

"Good morning," she replied, unable to hold back a smile. He was wearing impeccable beige linen slacks, a finely striped shirt, a pink cashmere pullover, and a patterned blue silk ascot. His charm was as thick and smooth as the fish purée. It brought out the worst in her: a sarcastic sense of humor.

"You must put on an apron," she said, handing him one, "or you'll spot your clothes."

He laughed, of course, at the absurdity of it. "*Mille fois merci*, but I don't think I'll be approaching the food until it's cooked." Another disarming smile. He walked over to

Daniel and the two men chatted quietly.

Vincent hauled over a small bin of apples and proffered a paring knife to anyone who was willing. Mr. Okura and Mr. Takashi didn't make a move; neither did Stuart or Patti.

"Looks like it's us," Barbara said to Richard and the Perkins.

"Can't be much different than peeling spuds," said George.

Gérard lined up two deep pie pans and slathered them inside with butter. As soon as an apple was peeled, he cored it, sliced it, sprinkled it with lemon juice, and tossed it in a bowl. He took down a canister of flour from the cabinet, and began the pastry – *pâte ordinaire* – which would be placed on top of the apples rather than underneath. Then the entire *tarte* would be flipped over after baking, like an upside-down cake. Gérard always liked to have an audience for this, and hear the admiring gasps when the cake pan was lifted off and the *tarte* appeared like a golden crown – high, puffy apples bathed in a caramel sauce.

With the *tartes Tatins* tucked into the oven, Gérard returned to the *quenelles*.

"Quenelles can be served with any number of sauces," explained Sybil. "A lot depends on what fish you've used to make them. With *brochet* – pike, that is – Gérard likes to serve a sauce Nantua."

Gérard had gotten a head start on this, having cooked some crayfish the night before. Now, he made a basic Béchamel sauce, cooked it down to half its volume, and added the crayfish stock and some cream, a little brandy, and a pinch of cayenne. He tasted it critically; everyone seemed to hold their breath until he nodded his approval.

Gérard put the sauce on a low burner to stay warm, and signaled Vincent that it was time to get back to the rabbit. Vincent brought over the bowl of marinating meat and he and Gérard removed the pieces, one by one, and dried them with a clean towel. Gérard put a large copper casserole on the fire and poured in a good shot of olive oil. He scooped a mound of flour onto the counter, and they both began rolling the pieces of rabbit into it and throwing them into the oil to brown. It was a long and tedious operation; Barbara began leafing through the recipes absentmindedly, and George and Richard strolled out to the herb garden. Patti leaned her chair against a wall and practiced the breathing exercises she had learned at a Hatha Yoga weekend in Palo Alto.

"No fair sleeping," Stefano purred in her ear.

She lurched forward, startled. Then she smiled apologetically.

"Honest, I wasn't sleeping. It was my deep breathing energizing exercise."

"Your what?," Stefano asked, amused.

"An energizing exercise I learned last spring at a weekend workshop. You try to breathe into your feet."

"Sounds wonderful for your feet," he said, with a mocking smile.

"Oh, it's not just for your feet," Patti said earnestly. "The energy only starts there, and then it works its way up."

"How far up?, Stefano asked, scanning her slowly from her pink shoes to her lavender tee-shirt.

Patti suddenly realized he was flirting, in what she thought must be a sophisticated European way. The men she met back home were very different, much more direct, and they would certainly know what deep breathing exercises were. Confused, but pleased at Stefano's attention, she pursued the conversation.

"Well, actually, it goes from the feet up through the legs and into the stomach, and then into the chest."

That was exactly where he was looking.

"Doesn't it ever get into your pretty little head?"

Patti, for once in her life, blushed.

"Well, there are other exercises for that. It's a different kind of breath."

He looked languidly into her eyes now.

"Ah, you Americans. You have techniques for everything." He brushed a strand of hair away from her eyes. "You turn everything natural into a formula, and then you have to smoke grass or sniff coke to get the natural feelings back again."

Patti was startled, not by the idea he expressed – which she wasn't sure she understood – but by his vocabulary. How did he know about grass and coke?

"Oh, we don't do it that much," she ventured. "Just to chill out now and then." She wondered if Stefano had any stuff on him. Stuart had brought over an ounce of coke, concealed in a can of talc, because he said he didn't know where to get it in Europe. But that was almost all gone now. She decided not to ask, not right away. She changed the subject. "Are you enjoying the course?"

Stefano looked vaguely into the distance. "It's too early to say." He looked into her eyes again. "It all depends on what develops."

She tried to think of an answer that was both nonchalant and encouraging, but Sybil's voice rang out triumphantly.

"*Voilà!* All the meat is browned. Now gather round and watch the next step."

George and Richard came in from the garden, and the Japanese huddled close to take some pictures. Gérard poured the marinade into the casserole, added some beef stock (a supply was always on hand in the fridge), and poured in enough wine to cover the meat. He turned up the flame to bring it to a boil, and then lowered the flame so it could simmer gently.

"About one and a half hours," said Sybil.

Next, Vincent brought over a basket of mushrooms and a bag of small white onions. Everyone was set to work again, stemming and rinsing the mushrooms and peeling the onions. Quickly, Gérard sautéed them in a large pan of butter, and set them aside. Then he returned to the *quenelles* and the Nantua sauce, which he stirred vigorously. His hand on the whisk was a sheer marvel, a kind of human appliance, moving in a rapid "8" pattern that clicked softly against the sides of the saucepan. He seemed tireless. Barbara watched him raptly.

"You want to try?", he smiled, almost indulgently.

"Uh, yes" she replied. She knew the motion, and although her tempo was slower, she was good. He nodded approvingly.

"Barbara's a great cook," Richard whispered to George and Helen. "When she puts her mind to it, she can really turn out a gourmet dinner."

"Helen's not bad herself," George said, "but she's never tried this fancy stuff."

"Maybe I will," Helen said, "if I can find something quick and easy."

Stuart shuffled over to Patti, who was looking distracted again.

"What'd Casanova have to say?", he asked.

"Oh, not much." She looked sleepy, or dreamy. "He's sort of a nice guy."

"Nice guys don't drive red Ferraris," Stuart said.

Had she detected a hint of jealousy? She was glad, so she plumped his pride a bit.

"How about guys who drive white Corvettes?"

"They're the greatest," grinned Stuart.

The sauce had thickened perfectly; it was *terminée*, announced Sybil. Gérard placed it on a warming plaque. He went to the wall oven and peeked in at the *tartes*, removed one, and tilted it to examine the sauce that ran out.

"If it's still light and liquidy, like this," explained Sybil, "the *tarte* isn't done. It has to bake long enough to caramelize to a nice, deep gold."

Gérard put the *tarte* back in the oven and set the timer for ten minutes.

"We can have our *apéritif* now," said Sybil, as if the *tarte* had obligingly agreed to wait. This was a treat, she knew, as the morning drew to an end and everyone was starting to feel restless and tired. Colette brought in a tray of glasses and Vincent opened two bottles of Condrieu.

"This is a very special white wine," said Sybil. "It doesn't really go with any food, so it's best just drunk alone, as an apéritif or a refresher."

The Japanese liked it; it felt thick and syrupy like sake. The Silvers, Patti, and Stuart made favorable murmurs, while the Perkins remained silent.

"It's an eccentric little wine," said Stefano, who knew it, of course. "Rather like a proud and lovely woman who can't relate to the world around her." He took another sip. "Very special."

Gérard looked at him dubiously. Who was this preposterous *personnage*? A *poseur*. A *séducteur* who was past his prime.

Sybil passed around some cheese straws that had been made with leftover pastry from yesterday's cheese puffs. She was amused by Stefano's comment, and wished, in a way, that she were a little more like that kind of woman: beautiful, mysterious, aloof.

"You're looking very mysterious," said Stefano, as he picked up a straw. Sybil, startled, laughed nervously.

"Oh, no. Just thinking about tomorrow's marketing." Lies and excuses. Why hadn't she ever learned the art of *bonne repartie*?

Daniel and the Silvers strolled out to the herb garden and stood for a while chatting on the patio. But suddenly Gérard's voice boomed out: *Vite! Tout le monde, venez!* The *tartes Tatins* were done. Deftly, he ran a knife around the crust, placed a serving plate over the cake pan, and flipped it over. There were gasps of admiration: each *tarte* slipped out golden and luscious, the apples puffed up high into a crown, glazed with the thick syrup.

"I'll never bake an apple pie again," sighed Barbara.

"That's mighty impressive," agreed George. Mr. Okura and Mr. Takashi clicked away.

"God, the calories there must be in that," said Patti.

Gérard put the *tartes* on racks to cool, and turned his attention to the *quenelles*. He set a pan of water on the stove to boil, salted it lightly, and gave the fish *purée* a final stir. Sybil explained that the purée would be dropped by spoonfuls into the boiling water (held to a low boil, Gérard specified), allowed to poach for about four minutes, lifted out with a slotted spatula, and drained on a tea towel. They would be placed on small toasted rounds of bread (Vincent was toasting them now, in a pan of butter), and served with a light gloss of Nantua sauce.

Gérard let everyone try poaching the *quenelles*. They didn't do badly, although George was a bit heavy-handed. Richard's movements were sure and studied – you knew he was a surgeon. Patti's *quenelle* slipped off the spatula and splashed back into the bubbling water, splattering her tee-shirt.

"I told you to wear your apron," Stuart grumbled. Stefano, as expected, declined the experience.

Alors, said Gérard, "we are almost ready to eat." He returned to the pot of rabbit and tested the meat for doneness with a fork. It was tender. Vincent, right on signal, came over with another deep pot and a sieve. He placed it in front of Gérard and then, grabbing the handles with a thick towel, he lifted the pot of *lapin* and slowly poured the liquid into the sieve. Gérard stirred it, slowly and carefully, pressing through the onions and carrots.

"That adds flavor to the sauce, of course," explained Sybil, "but it also helps thicken it."

Everyone crowded around the counter to watch. The odor was intoxicating: a perfect blend of Burgundy wine, meat and vegetables, sparked by just enough garlic and thyme.

Colette came in to set the long oak table. Sybil gave her a hand, placing the forks the French way – tines down – and folding a big checkered napkin across every plate. There was a hungry rustle of excitement. Even the Japanese – delicate, small-boned men – looked ravenous. Patti ran upstairs to change her tee-shirt, and George and Daniel pulled over the chairs. Six were lined up on either side, plus one at either end for Sybil and Gérard.

"This is one place where I'm not the man of the house," Daniel grinned at George.

George patted him on the back. "Don't let it become a habit, fella."

Antoine came in with the wine: a Muscadet for the *quenelles* and a Crozes Hermitage for the rabbit. He smiled and nodded *"Bonjour"* to everyone, and began uncorking the bottles. His English was not much better than Gérard's, but with his heavy, delightful accent, he explained his choice for the meal.

Patti returned with her hair freshly combed, wearing a clean pink tee-shirt that said "Foxy Lady" across the back. Sybil motioned for everyone to sit down. Stefano quickly surveyed the table and placed himself next to Barbara, at Sybil's right. Stuart and Patti sat across from him. George and Helen came next, across from Daniel. The Japanese, Antoine, and Vincent flanked Gérard.

"Thank heavens, an even fourteen," thought Sybil. While Antoine passed around the wine, Gérard and Vincent arranged the *quenelles* on individual plates. Colette served them, starting with Sybil.

"It seems you're the court taster," Stefano said to her. "Will you have the first nibble, and assure us they're not poisoned?"

"No danger of that," Sybil laughed. "We're more likely to die of over-consumption."

"I wonder how often a court taster actually died," mused Barbara. "You never read about that in the history books."

"Of course not," said Stefano. "The only lives that counted were the lords they were serving. Now today, in our own time, in our democratic western civilization, anyone's death is important. A tramp can freeze to death on the street, and the media will blow it up into headline news. Which means, perversely, that we're more interested in death as a phenomenon than in the individual as a person."

"Oh, that's not true," Richard protested. "I think we recognize that everyone's life is important, whether it's a tramp who dies or a president."

"Oh, come now," said Stefano, happy to have aroused some discussion. "In the first place, the president of a nation is not likely to die of cold in the gutter. The kind of death he experiences – be it assassination, a plane crash, or something as mundane as a heart attack – is far less the issue than the fact that he is dead. There is suddenly a vacuum, a space to be filled, a new realignment of power. When a tramp dies, not one ripple is felt in the world. It is only, possibly, the unusual circumstances of his death that are interesting."

"But he's still a human being," insisted Richard.

"Of course, he *was* a human being. But a far less significant one."

"But significance isn't what counts." Richard's voice was rising.

Stefano smiled to himself, recognizing the typical American knee-jerk reaction: the sanctity of life, any life, and that blind egalitarianism, the great leveler.

"My dear friend," he said, "significance does count. Quite honestly, if two dying men were brought to you for a life-saving operation, one a derelict from the Bowery and the other a world-renowned musician, which one would you choose to save?"

"Those are the choices we're faced with all the time, one way or the other," answered Richard.

"Well, how do you solve them?", pursued Stefano, ruthlessly.

"Well, there are all kinds of factors to be considered..."

"Nonsense," interrupted Stefano. "The bottom line is

always, 'Whose life is more valuable?' The octogenarian or the young child? The mailroom clerk or the chairman of the board? The spinster or the mother of five? Don't tell me you disregard rank and social function when you make these decisions."

"These *quenelles* are delicious." Barbara blurted out. It was hardly a subtle way to change the conversation but she knew she had to do something or Richard would rise from the table in a rage. Sometimes, at dinner parties in New York he would be drawn into discussions like this, usually by lawyers and sociologists. She knew how impossible it was to explain his ethical position even to himself. It always sounded pompous and pretentious or absurdly naive. She knew, too, the torment he went through every time such a decision had to be made and how he tried desperately to view every life as supremely important and worthy of saving. Even the hopeless cases, the terminally ill, the comatose, the vegetables.

Sybil quickly picked up on Barbara's cue. She also felt the conversation had gone too far.

"Yes. The touch of crayfish in the sauce is such a nice complement to the pike. And the contrast of the smooth *quenelle* with the crisp toast is delightful."

Stefano realized his train of argument had just been derailed by the two women. How very Anglo-Saxon. A French woman would have made a witty or outrageous remark, which would have raised the level of discussion to some airless abstract plane or simply have shrunk it to the proportions of a joke. He sighed inaudibly. This was going to be a very dull week. Fortunately, Lucinda was arriving on Wednesday.

He turned to Sybil and asked her if she had any word from Signora Contini.

"Yes, I have. She said she's very sorry to be missing the first few days, but will be here at tea-time on Wednesday."

Stefano smiled. Tea-time, indeed. Lucinda never drank tea after ten in the morning. What she was saying, if Sybil only knew, was that she'd arrive in time for cocktails.

"I believe she's driving over from Geneva," Sybil continued.

Stefano nodded. Geneva was only two hours away, over the Franco-Swiss border. Lucinda would make it in about an hour and a half in her Alfa Romeo. He remembered the last time he had driven with her, from Lake Como to Milan. They had had lunch at the Villa d'Este in Cernobbio, had drunk two bottles of Valpolicella, ordered two expressos with sambucco, and finished that off with some lacrima Cristi. He had offered to do the driving, but Lucinda wouldn't hear of it.

"How would it look if we had an accident and a strange man was found behind the wheel of my car?"

"Would it be any different if you had an accident and a strange man was found next to you in the car?," he had asked, quite logically.

"Certainly," she said. "I could always pass you off as a hitchhiker."

Which, in a way, I am, he thought wryly: personal assistant and financial advisor to Cosimo Contini, and surrogate bed partner to his wife. Anyway, Lucinda had taken the wheel that day, had careened around the narrow streets of Lugano, and had maintained a cruising speed of 170 kilometers an hour all the way down the Autostrada del Sole, back to Milan. He admired her nerve, but he nearly lost his own, especially when she took one hand off the wheel to puff on a cigarette. He was sober and grateful when she dropped him off in front of his apartment on the Via Manzoni.

Mia cara, he said, kissing her goodbye on the cheek, "didn't you ever take driver's training courses in high school?"

"Never," she said. "My brothers taught me how to drive. All over Pittsburgh. We were known as the terrible three."

"That explains it," he smiled, patting her cheek. "You've had an incomplete education."

"I went to the school of hard knocks," she said cockily. "That means more than all your fancy European diplomas."

Maybe it does, thought Stefano, but thank God he had the fancy diplomas. Without them, where would he be today? Just another poor man with a title on his calling card.

Colette was clearing away the dishes from the first course, and Gérard was correcting the seasoning of the rabbit.

"You never put in salt at the beginning of cooking," explained Sybil with great care, "because the liquid evaporates and the salt doesn't, so you end up with too much salt. Always, always add salt at the end."

Barbara pulled out the recipes from her big canvas bag and scribbled down the advice. Stefano glanced at her, then looked across the table at Patti and Stuart. They were practically billing and cooing. Stuart had his arm around her chair, and they were talking softly, their heads close together. Wonderful what a little wine can do, Stefano reflected, as Patti picked a thread off Stuart's green Lacoste shirt. They're already in the mood for a siesta.

Daniel was trying to make conversation with the Japanese. He was asking about the hotel chain they represented, and what the company's plans were for expanding in Europe. He didn't get very far. Either they truly didn't understand him, or they were being cleverly evasive. Okay, he thought, have it your way. I can ring up the office this evening and have Paula check it out, this mysterious Mitohashi Group.

The *lapin* was served, pungent and steaming. Antoine poured the Hermitage. The bread basket was passed around and Sybil urged everyone to take a slice: "Don't worry about your manners. You have to wipe up every drop of sauce."

And they did, self-consciously at first. George asked for more bread, and Daniel, too, decided what the hell – next week he'd be back to New York salad bars – and he had another portion. Barbara wondered if d'Agostino's carried rabbit, or if she could substitute chicken in a pinch. She questioned Richard: he said he thought Central Park squirrels would do quite nicely. Barbara grimaced in mock disgust.

"Doctor Silver, you have an uncanny sense of the grotesque and the unappetizing." She felt Stefano fumbling on the floor for his napkin. His hand grazed her ankle. She jumped slightly and turned to him, just as he was rising with the napkin in his hand.

"Sorry," he said. "What were you saying about squirrels?"

"My husband was saying they might be a good substitute for rabbit."

"Why not?", said Stefano, putting the napkin back on his lap. "During the war, we ate anything that hopped, crawled or flew."

"Yes, I've read that the European cat population was nearly decimated, and animals were even slaughtered in the zoos," Richard added. The provocation of a few moments ago was forgotten.

Stefano nodded gravely.

"Where were you during the war?", Barbara asked. "Italy?"

"Oh, here and there," Stefano answered, still gravely. "We had to keep two steps ahead of the Germans."

"Like everyone else," said Daniel. "I've met so many Europeans – well, almost everyone over fifty – who have stories to tell about the war. This region right here was hard hit, wasn't it, Gérard?"

Gérard looked up from the counter, where he was slicing the *tartes Tatin*.

Eh, oui, he said. "The Germans occupied most of Burgundy. The officers and their staffs took over some of the châteaux. They took food away from the farmers and made the local people work for them, like slaves."

"Were there many collaborators?," asked Richard. He remembered post-war French films where collaborators were shot and women who had taken Nazi lovers had their heads shaved.

Gérard was silent. Then he said softly, "Even a few is too many." He would say no more. Sybil broke in again to save another awkward situation.

"The Resistance fighters were marvelous. Truly admirable. Gérard's father was a local commander. Antoine's father, too. They coordinated their activities with the Resistance groups up in Paris and out in Normandy."

Gérard brought the *tartes* over to the table. They were still warm. He set a large bowl of *crème fraîche* next to them.

"Were your fathers decorated after the war?," Richard asked.

"Yes, posthumously." Gérard glanced at Antoine, who was staring into his wineglass.

Sybil made another attempt to brighten the conversation.

"Now then, let's pass around the *tartes*. Mr. Takashi, will you start, and send it down this side, and Mr. Okura, will you start on the other side? Don't forget the *crème fraîche*. It's gilding the lily, in a way, and really quite sinful. But it is delicious."

This time it worked. There were murmurs of contentment, and the war was dismissed.

Daniel admired Sybil's skill; he had seen it often. She was as deft as she was determined, and had saved, single-handedly, a number of dinner parties back home from degenerating into disaster. When possible, she even used her English façade as a shield to deflect the disputes. Someone was ranting about the rising number of welfare cases? "Oh, my, if you knew what socialized medicine costs us in Great Britain." A Republican and a Democrat were at each other's throats? "You know, this reminds me so much of arguments between the Conservatives and Labour." Then she would pass the raspberry sauce or ring for the maid to come and clear the table.

She was ringing now for Colette to come and serve the coffee.

Stuart and Patti excused themselves; they really had too much to drink, they said, and needed a little nap. Helen warned George to go easy on the sugar; he had enough calories for the day. Daniel yawned, rose from the table, and told Vincent he'd see him in half an hour on the tennis court. Stefano turned to Barbara and Richard and asked if they played backgammon; he had noticed a board in the salon. Richard said yes, but Barbara begged off: "I think I need some fresh air after that gluttonous meal." Mr Takashi and Mr. Okura said they would walk into the town and leave some films for developing. Sybil was glad no one asked for anything special, like a hairdresser's appointment or a ride to Beaune to get the newspapers. That would come, she knew, later in the week, when things got more routine.

She chatted a few moments with Gérard.

"That was a splendid lunch," she said.

Comme d'habitude, said Antoine.

"Yes, as usual," agreed Sybil, "but even better than usual. Gérard, what on earth did you do to the *Tatin* to make it so light?"

Gérard smiled slyly as he removed his toque. Naturally, Sybil would notice every nuance, even a different texture in the apples.

Ma chère Madame, he grinned, "I simply put the oven temperature a few degrees higher at the start, only for ten minutes. It gave an extra puff to the *pommes.*"

Sybil shook her head. "You cheat, you know. You do things behind our backs. So it becomes impossible to duplicate your genius."

"But that's what genius is all about," said Gérard, who would never refuse an honest compliment. "It's keeping several jumps ahead of everyone else. *N'est-ce pas,* Antoine?"

Absolument, he said. "Except when it's the genius of keeping several steps behind."

"Incorrigible," laughed Sybil, "both of you." She plucked two zinnias from the centerpiece and popped them in their breast pockets.

* * *

Patti squirmed under Stuart's leaden arm, and for a moment wondered why the room was so bright. Then she remembered it was mid-afternoon. Stuart, as always after lovemaking, had sunk into a heavy sleep. Patti had only slept lightly, briefly, and her right hand, immobilized under Stuart's chest, was numb. Got to get up, she thought, and she nudged him firmly to roll over. He did, without a break in his breathing.

She went into the bathroom, shaking her wrist to get the circulation going again. She looked in the mirror and saw her mascara had made stripes down her cheeks. She never liked making love in the middle of the day, but Stuart had been so excited and insistent that she readily gave in. She was glad she could still arouse him that way, even if it wasn't her preferred timing, and even if he came too fast and left her high and dry. That happened often, she thought ruefully, except when they'd been snorting coke and she was feeling high.

"Well, what do you expect after four years of living together?," her friend Vicky asked. "You're like an old married couple by now."

Except that they weren't an old married couple, Patti reflected miserably; not even a young married couple. Not a married couple at all, but two people who had settled into an easy pattern, and who found it easier to hang on to that pattern than to split. In back of her mind, and maybe in back of Stuart's mind, too, was the idea that someone might come along some day and offer something still easier. Then what?

Patti took a washcloth and wiped away the mascara. Then she dabbed her whole face with lotion and began to re-do the entire make-up. It was a bore. It was so much nicer when she was doing a modeling assignment or a TV commercial, and a make-up man would work over her face completely, putting just the right amount of shading under the chin, the right amount of gloss on the lips, the right hue of blue along the eyelids. The powder puff slipped from her hand and fell into a puddle in the washbasin. "Damn," she muttered, and finished powdering with a cotton ball.

She looked at herself in profile in the long bathroom mirror as she brushed and teased her hair. The curves were filling out more than they should, she mused. She'd have to put in extra time at the gym when they got back to L.A.

"Some day, Patti Olsen," she sighed to herself, "you're going to have lots of babies and get very fat and eat whatever you want and not do a stitch of exercise and not have anyone look at you and you're not going to care." It sounded like heaven.

She slipped back into her Foxy Lady tee-shirt, and pulled on a pair of shorts and some white sandals. She scribbled a note for Stu: Gone for a stroll. See you in the kitchen at 4.

Downstairs, she peered into the salon and saw Stefano leafing through a wine encyclopedia. He had changed into white slacks and a blue silk shirt. He looked up and smiled broadly.

"Hello, there. Have a good siesta?"

She smiled back self-consciously. He might as well have said, "Have a good screw?"

"Yes, thank you. I really needed a nap after that huge lunch."

"Of course," he said. "When you're not used to eating and drinking like that in the middle of the day, it affects you."

"I'll have to go on a diet after a week here," she nodded.

"Oh, it's not a question of pounds," said Stefano, with the air of an elder statesman. "It's a matter of distribution. A young woman like you seems to keep everything very well distributed."

She looked at him, not comprehending.

"You know. Well proportioned."

At last Patti caught on, and realized this was again his European way of chatting her up.

"Well, I think I need some exercise anyway. I'm going to go for a little walk."

"Do you know your way around?," Stefano asked. "Perhaps I should accompany you." He rose briskly from his chair.

"Oh, no, that's all right," Patti demurred.

"No, really, it will be a pleasure for me. You missed the formal tour yesterday, so I'll give you an informal one now."

He took her arm and led her out the front door.

Okay, Patti thought. He's old enough to be my father, but he sure has style.

Stefano followed Sybil's route exactly: the *poulailler*, the storage room, the press, the barn, the stables, and around the back of the château to the tennis court and garden.

"Too bad there's no swimming pool," said Patti.

"Oh, the French aren't great swimmers," said Stefano. "They're frogs, you know. They just jump around a bit and get their feet wet. Anyway, the summers usually aren't hot enough here to make a pool worthwhile."

"You're Italian, aren't you?," Patti asked.

"In part," Stefano replied. "You might say I'm a blend

of the best and the worst of Europe. Most of the time, I hope, the Italian dominates."

"Have you ever been to the United States?," Patti queried, realizing at once that of course he must have been. "Naturally, many times."

"For business or pleasure?" These were dumb questions, but she was trying to keep the conversation impersonal. He had taken her arm again.

"Well, to tell you the truth, my business is a pleasure, and my pleasure is serious business, so I can't really answer your question, can I? Life sometimes gets mixed up like that."

"I know what you mean. Stu is crazy about his work. He gets a real high when he wins a case. He's got one of the fastest growing law offices in the county." Her sudden loyalty to Stuart surprised her. She actually hated the way his work ate up his time.

"But does he play hard, too?," asked Stefano, squeezing her arm imperceptibly.

"Oh, sure. Squash, jogging, windsurfing. All that."

"Ah, the beautiful life in California," smiled Stefano. "And what about you? You're an actress?"

"Not yet. Not exactly. I mean, I'm a model. I don't know if I'll ever have an acting career."

"Why not? Have you studied acting?"

"A little. Some studio acting classes and all that."

"So why not?"

"Well, you know, it's hard. Everybody out there wants to act. The competition is terrible." She didn't like all these questions about her "career". She'd been knocking on doors since she was seventeen.

"I'm sure a young woman like you has only to knock on a door and name her price," said Stefano. "In a manner of speaking."

She shot him a glance; what exactly did he mean? But he was holding open the gate and playfully tugging on her hand.

"Come on. I'll show you the sexiest little vineyard in Burgundy."

*   *   *

Daniel was humming loudly in the shower.

"Have a good match, dear?", Sybil called from the bed. He didn't hear her, so she waited until he came out. "Did you have a good match, dear?"

"Not bad," he answered, rubbing the towel across his back. "Vincent will never be a great player, but he's okay. Too bad he didn't start earlier in life."

"Well, tennis didn't really catch on in France until very recently, you know. It was always such an elitist sport. You remember how I had to wrangle with Gérard to get the court built."

"Good thing it's there. Next thing you've got to get him to do is put in a swimming pool."

"That will be harder," sighed Sybil, stretching out on the bed. "The construction, the maintenance....you know how Gérard hangs on to his *sous*."

"That's the main problem here, Syb," Daniel continued.

"No business sense, no foresight. Why, this place and all the châteaux in Burgundy are an untapped goldmine. With some solid investment and some good management, this area could become another Loire Valley."

"It's becoming that quite fast enough," said Sybil. "I certainly wouldn't hurry the process."

"Syb," said Daniel, sitting down on the edge of the bed, his voice suddenly earnest, "what do you think about selling St.-Cloud? To a major international conglomerate that would develop it the way it should be developed?"

Sybil raised her head from the pillow and looked at him in amazement.

"What are you saying, Daniel?"

Daniel took a deep breath, knowing he was treading on sensitive ground, as he had known for months he would be.

"Look, I've been in contact with a big Italian group that wants to purchase eight or ten châteaux in this area. Their idea is to combine the resources, consolidate the vineyards, make a real business out of this, the way it's done in Bordeaux. I think they're on the right track."

"But this *isn't* Bordeaux," said Sybil, propping herself up on an elbow.

"But it could be," insisted Daniel. "Hell, look at what you've got now – five thousand individual proprietors eking out their existence on a mere 12,000 acres. Practically living from hand to mouth, year to year, never knowing if it's going to be a dream of a harvest or a disaster. Who guard their two or three little acres as if it's the end of the world. Now, with one owner operating eight or ten of these *domaines*, you spread the risk. The result is higher profitability, more reinvestment, bigger production, and better business all around."

Sybil stared at him, dumbstruck.

"Daniel, are you promoting this idea?"

"The Contini group is promoting this idea, and I'm helping them get it off the ground." He said it firmly, sternly.

"They're your clients?"

"Right. I'm giving them my legal and financial expertise."

"Why are you involving St.-Cloud?"

"That's the place I know best, isn't it? All the problems I see here are duplicated, in one way or another, in every château and vineyard in the region."

"But you're taking advantage of my position here, and Gérard's friendship!" Sybil sensed, with alarm, Daniel's determination; she had seen it emerge many times before, but in its proper place, on Wall Street. Here, it seemed monstrous.

"Sybil, that's the point." He put her hand on hers. "You, better than anyone else, can convince Gérard to sell. Once he sells, the neighbors will start considering it. Then it's only a matter of time."

"You're asking me to betray him," Sybil said, sitting now on the edge of the bed and clutching it. "And Vincent, too."

"Oh, you don't have to worry about Vincent," said Daniel. "I've broached the subject to him and he sees the advantages. He'd be allowed to stay on as general manager."

"And Antoine?"

"I guess he could stay on during the transition, and be gradually phased out."

"I just can't believe it," said Sybil. "It's all so coldblooded. This is a family place, not a factory."

"Sybil, it won't be a factory. The name will stay. The quality will stay. Only it will finally become a stable, profitable, rational business."

"Like a Scotch distillery. Or a pizza parlor." Suddenly, Sybil realized why Stefano di Carozza was there. "Carozza, he's with this group?"

"Yes; he's their financial manager."

"And this Contini woman who's coming on Wednesday?"

"She's the boss' wife."

Sybil rose quickly and went to the bathroom to wash up.

"Syb, can I count on you to talk it over with Gérard?"

There was no answer.

"Syb?"

She came out of the bathroom, wiping her hands on a towel.

"Yes, I'll talk it over with Gérard, and I'll tell him he'd be a bloody fool to sell."

Daniel heaved a sigh, exasperated.

"You're being too goddam sentimental, Syb. I'm sure if you approached Gérard in the right way, he'd see the advantages of it. He can't keep this place going many more years, and when he sees Vincent is in favor..."

"Vincent would turn this place over to Walt Disney if it meant more money for him." She folded the towel and hung it back on the rack. "No, Daniel, don't count on me to butter up Gérard for this one. You and Carozza can try your luck alone."

Daniel ran a hand through his hair. Thinning and graying, he thought. Dammit, why couldn't Sybil see straight? He realized now she would do everything in her power to turn Gérard against the proposal. His only remaining hope was Vincent.

*　　*　　*

George hurried over to Sybil as soon as he saw her coming down the stairs.

"Missus Dickson," he drawled, "I hate to bother you but I've gotta make a call to my office today."

"We can arrange that," said Sybil, still upset from her talk with Daniel but determined not to show it. She had to get through the demonstration class, and speak to Gérard right after.

"Problem is," said George, "I don't know what the time difference is between here and Texas."

Sybil reflected. Was Texas on Central Time, like Chicago? Yes, she thought so.

"They're seven hours behind us, I think."

"Let's see. That'll make it almost nine in the morning. That'll be fine. Gotta get them moving on some projects this week."

Sybil had learned the local peculiarities – the *tics*, as the

French would say – of every region in America, and she even felt comfortable with many of them. She loved the cultured crustiness of New England, the sugared hospitality of the South, the laid-back hedonism of California, and the earthy naïveté of the Middle West. But she never, never understood Texas.

"They're like overgrown children," she once told Daniel, after a gastronomic lecture tour in Houston, Dallas and San Antonio. "Or under-grown adults."

She had the same feeling facing George – a sweet, well-meaning man who couldn't wrench himself away from his insurance business for a week; who carried Dallas with him wherever he went.

George noticed she had fallen silent, and thought she must be worried about the cost of the call.

"Don't worry," he quickly said, "I'm making it a collect call."

"Oh, that's fine," said Sybil, snapping out of her reverie.

"I'll show you how to do it. Come on up to my office."

She rang up the operator, said she wanted to make a call *en PCV aux Etats-Unis*, and asked George for the number.

"You've got a fine command of French," he said, although he didn't understand a word.

Sybil smiled. "I've still got an awful British accent."

"You've got that even when you speak English," grinned George.

Sybil laughed, and handed him the receiver. "Here's your office," she said, and left the room.

Downstairs, the guests were assembling for the demonstration course.

"Everyone into the kitchen," she said crisply. Patti, looking distraught and disheveled, said she had to go wake up Stuart. Helen said she'd wait for George to finish his call. Barbara and Richard ambled in, trailing the eager Japanese. Where was Stefano? Sybil didn't want to encounter him right now; just as well if he didn't show up.

Daniel was already in the kitchen, talking softly to Vincent. Gérard was laying out the produce and the utensils for the first recipe: a *Turban de Truite et Saumon*. It was a magnificent dish, and Sybil wished she felt in a more festive mood for it. She sat down sadly on her high stool near the counter, and fiddled with the fine-bladed boning knife.

S'il te plait, said Gérard, holding out his hand, and she passed him the knife. He began preparing the whiting, the trout, and the salmon that would make up the *mousseline*. Then, with another knife, he carved equal quantities of fresh salmon and smoked salmon into thin slices. Carefully, as if he were dressing a wound, he lined a large copper ring mold with alternate slices of the salmon, after slathering the mold with butter. Then he took the other fish and piled it into a food processor with some softened butter. When it was puréed, he forced the mixture through a sieve, into a large bowl set in a larger bowl of ice. He stirred in two egg yolks, one egg white, some heavy cream, and salt and pepper. In another bowl, he beat several egg whites into soft peaks, and folded that into the fish mixture.

Helen and George came in, looking worried. They sat

down behind the Silvers, and Sybil noticed Helen gently pat George's hand, reassuringly. You're not the only ones with problems, Sybil thought.

She realized the demonstration had been going on without her usual commentary, so she pulled herself together and with some effort focused on the fish.

"You must never use frozen fish for this," she warned. "Fish that's been frozen has lost its gluten, and the *mousseline* won't hold together."

Gérard was now poaching a spoonful of the *mousseline* mixture in boiling water. "That's how you can sample it and see if the seasoning needs to be corrected," Sybil explained. Gérard lifted the little patty out of the water with his slotted spoon, waited a moment, and tasted it. Everyone watched, awaiting his verdict. He nodded his approval. *C'est bon.* Heads have rolled and kingdoms have tottered for less than that, thought Sybil. A pinch of salt, or a golden thread, or a horseshoe nail. It's all so precarious. She wanted to cry.

Gérard spooned the *mousseline* mixture into the center of the mold, and folded the salmon slices over the top. He covered it all with buttered foil, and simmered the mold in a pan of water on top of the stove.

"You can prepare it in advance, up to this point"' said Sybil. "Just keep it in the fridge until you're ready to cook it."

After a few minutes, Gérard lifted the mold out of the water and put it in the oven.

"It will bake now for about 35 to 45 minutes," said Sybil, "and then you can keep it in a warm place for up to half an hour before serving it."

There was a rustle, and Patti shuffled in, followed by Stuart. She looked sulky, he looked sullen. Sybil thought they had probably had a spat.

"Sorry you missed this," she said, trying to sound sorry. "It's a *tour de force* – a real masterpiece."

Patti murmured something, and took a seat near the window. Stuart folded his arms and leaned against the wall. Barbara glanced at them, saw what was going on, and leaned over to Richard. "Young lovers."

Sybil sensed that interest was lagging. Her head was starting to throb, and she wanted to get the demonstration over with quickly so she could talk to Gérard. But there was still the pastry to be made – the *feuilleté aux fraises*. Gérard had already poured four cups of flour onto his marble pastry slab, and was cutting in two cups of butter. Eventually, it became a granular mixture, and he added a cup of cold water. "Cold," emphasized Sybil. "Everything has to be cold." A pinch of salt, and the dough was patted into a ball and popped in the refrigerator. "Chill it for half an hour." God, Sybil thought, I wish I had an ice bag for my head.

Vincent brought over four small boxes of strawberries and rinsed them quickly, while Gérard began the *crème pâtissière*. With a wire whisk, he beat together two egg yolks, 100 grams of sugar, and a packet of vanilla sugar. Gradually, he beat in 50 grams of sifted flour, and then a whole egg.

"The mixture gets almost white," explained Sybil.

Meanwhile, Vincent was bringing half a liter of milk to the boil, with a pinch of salt. When it reached the boil, Gérard poured it slowly into his egg mixture, still whisking furiously. Then he put it on the fire, and continued to beat it while bringing it to the boil three times.

"Why do you take it on and off like that?", asked Barbara, "instead of letting it boil a few minutes all at once?"

Sybil used to wonder about that, too. "It's to get it to the right temperature so it thickens, but it doesn't get overcooked. Kind of a safety valve."

It was finished. Gérard took it off the heat and poured in a splash of Grand-Marnier. That would enhance the flavor of the strawberries. Not missing a beat, he took the ball of pastry from the refrigerator, sprinkled some flour on the marble slab, and deftly rolled it out for the last time.

Daniel was looking at his watch. Six o'clock. He slipped out the door to the garden. At the far end of the counter, Vincent was duplicating what Gérard had done, in order to have a second *feuilleté* for dinner. Sybil often tried to compare Vincent's work with Gérard's, by tasting a little of both. She always favored Gérard's, but she knew it wasn't really a blind tasting, for she had watched them both like a hawk.

Daniel's gotten antsy, she thought. Where has he gone? She looked through the French doors and saw him waving to Stefano. The two men approached each other and strolled off. Sybil swallowed hard. They looked like conspirators.

Gérard opened the oven door to check the *turban*. It was ready. He removed it, and turned up the heat for the pastry shells.

Regardez bien, he said, and the class stared, transfixed. He tipped the mold carefully to pour off the excess liquid. Then he put a serving plate on top and swiftly flipped the mold over and lifted it off. There were gasps: it was a perfect crown of salmon, with alternating pale and dark orange stripes. Gérard could barely conceal his pride; it was one of his special dishes.

While Vincent tucked the pastry into the pie pans, Gérard took a saucepan to make the *Sauce Beurre Blanc* that would accompany the *turban*. He chopped four shallots, and boiled them in six tablespoons of dry white wine and white wine vinegar. When the liquid was reduced to less than half, he lowered the flame, sprinkled in some salt and white pepper, and whisked in a pound of butter, nugget by nugget.

"My God, the cholesterol," Barbara whispered to Richard. "That man uses butter as if it were going out of style."

"Hardly a dish I'd recommend to my patients," Richard nodded. "But it's funny about the French – they die from alcohol, not butter fat."

Sybil was explaining that the *beurre blanc* sauce can't be kept very long or it separates out, but it can be held for a little while over a pan of warm water, as Gérard was doing. Then, from the fridge, he took a bowl of baby shrimp and a black truffle.

Vous connaissez? he asked, holding it up. *Un diamant noir.*

"A black diamond, indeed," said Sybil to her audience. "Fresh truffles cost hundreds of dollars a pound. They say Louis XIV used to eat five pounds of them a day. They were believed to be an aphrodisiac."

"And indeed they are," said a voice behind her. It was

Stefano. "But there are so many other aphrodisiacs that are far less expensive."

Sybil wanted to ignore his interruption, but Helen, roused from her drowsiness, asked him for examples.

"Well, tomatoes for one thing. They were called love apples when explorers first brought them back to Europe from South America. It was forbidden to eat them for almost a century."

"Can you imagine the Italians without tomatoes?", reflected Barbara.

"Exactly," smiled Stefano. "The so-called Latin temperament may be no more than a question of cuisine. Imagine if the English ate more tomato sauce. I daresay they could use it."

Sybil winced but Barbara laughed. "What about the Americans?"

"That's a good case in point. The permissive society, the sexual revolution, the growing violence – you can trace it all to the diet of these past two decades. Big Macs smothered in ketchup."

"Ketchup!", exclaimed Barbara.

"Ketchup," purred Stefano. "The poor man's aphrodisiac. The opiate of the starving masses".

"Christ," chuckled Richard. "I'd better buy stock in H. J. Heinz."

Sybil cleared her throat and tapped on the countertop with a spoon. Colette had been setting the table for dinner, so she told everyone they could take a break, wash up, and return in fifteen minutes. Barbara stayed on to watch Gérard assemble the strawberry tarts, spooning the *crème patissière* into the baked pie shells and arranging the plump berries over it. Vincent had made a strawberry *glaçage* which was poured over the top as a glaze.

"Beautiful!", said Barbara.

Gérard smiled and winked at her. She was a pretty woman, he thought; smart, like most New York women, but without that sharp edge, that arrogant air. Sybil had told him she was a decorator, and that probably explained her interest in the château's architecture and furnishings.

"You have the artistic eye," he said, trying to muster his best English. But the *th* still came out *z*.

"Well, I'm an interior decorator. It's important to me how things look."

Il faut se méfier des apparences, said Stefano, hovering behind her. "Sorry – that means you have to beware of appearances." He beamed beguilingly. "But then again, what else have we to go on?"

"Oh, I don't know," said Barbara, searching for a clever answer. "Don't you look for character and integrity?"

"Of course," said Stefano, "but those things can so easily be simulated. You have to beware of them most of all. Now, when you see dishonesty and a *lack* of character, you can be sure it's true, because nobody would simulate that."

"Yes, I guess that's so," Barbara said, a bit confused and dazzled by his rapid reasoning. But she added, brightly, "I guess that makes you a cynic."

"Not all," said Stefano. "I'm a realist." Another broad smile.

Barbara didn't know what else to say. She felt as though she had been towed far out on a charming little lake and left there, without a paddle. So she simply smiled back.

Sybil returned with all the guests behind her. Daniel was in the rear, talking – or gesticulating – to the Japanese. Patti and Stuart still seemed sullen. Helen and George looked ready for a good meal. Richard walked over to Barbara and put his arm around her waist, as Stefano excused himself to go wash up. Sybil, before taking her place at the head of the table, went over to Gérard and whispered urgently in his ear: "Gérard, I must talk to you after dinner."

*　　*　　*

It was after ten o'clock, and an orange moon was rising over the low hills. Sybil sat on the terrace waiting for Gérard to finish his chores; she heard the clatter of heavy copper pans, and, intermittently, his whistling. There was almost a chill in the air; summer had turned the bend. She pulled the flowered Liberty scarf around her shoulders.

"Looks like a real harvest moon," said a drawling voice. It was George.

"Yes, it does," she answered, without much enthusiasm. Please go away, she thought.

"I oughta call Helen to come out and see this."

Please don't, she prayed.

"I bet we're gonna have a real Indian summer."

Not likely in Burgundy, she smirked silently. "No, that's very rare in France," she said politely.

"That's the best part of the year," he continued, as if

she hadn't answered. "The fishing's good, and the garden just keeps blooming forever."

Sybil tried to imagine George with a fishing pole, or garden shears. No, she could only see him driving a white Lincoln to a shopping center.

"Well, guess I'll turn in," he said. Was he really giving up on her? "Sleep good."

"Thank you," she replied. "Have a good night's sleep."

Silence again. It was a balm.

Finally, the kitchen door opened and Gérard came out. He sat down on the bench next to her and let out a long, satisfied sigh.

"Antoine and Vincent, they say goodnight and *à demain*," he said.

Merci, Sybil answered, glad that they had left. This had to be done alone with Gérard, *face à face*.

She took a deep breath. "Gérard, are you happy at St.-Cloud?"

He was startled by her question, and curious. Sybil only asked vague questions when she was about to embark on a serious discussion.

"Of course," he said, waiting for the dénouement.

"I mean, really happy. Do you feel it's your real home? Do you feel attached to it?"

"Of course," he said again. She wasn't getting to the point yet.

"Would you ever consider selling it?"

Voilà – that was it. He looked her straight in the eyes. "You want to buy it?"

"Oh God, no," she exclaimed. "I'm just wondering if you'd ever let it out of the family."

Back to vague questions. "Of course not," he replied.

"Gérard," – why was a lump rising in her throat? – "I think someone wants to take over St-Cloud. Buy it, I mean."

"Who?"

"An Italian group, an international conglomerate. They want to buy up acres of Burgundy vineyards, starting here."

"At St.-Cloud?"

"Yes," she shouted, as if he were being deliberately obtuse. No, take it easy, she thought. Naturally, he hasn't an inkling.

"Gérard," she said softly, almost conspiringly, "this Carozza character is their agent. It's the Contini group. Mrs. Contini, who's arriving Wednesday, is the boss' wife." She inhaled deeply. "And Daniel is their counsel."

"Daniel?" Daniel, to Gérard, was a kind of ghost – a twilight figure who appeared for two weeks a year, brandished a tennis racket, and left.

"Daniel is their counsel," Sybil repeated slowly, as if to impress it upon herself as well as Gérard.

Gérard was silent for a while, as he was when he was blending a sauce or trimming a cutlet. Then he exploded.

"*Incroyable*! I don't believe it!"

"It's true," Sybil insisted. "They want to get a foothold in Burgundy, buy up the small producers, consolidate the business, make it a big-time operation."

"And they want St.-Cloud?"

"Especially St.-Cloud. You're the key person here. You have the reputation. If you sell, they're sure everyone else will sell."

"How much do they offer?"

"Gérard! Are you saying you'd sell?"

"No. I'm just asking how much they offer. My curiosity wants to know what I'm worth."

"Honestly, I have no idea. I'm simply appalled at the whole concept."

Gérard shrugged. "It's already happening in Champagne. Maybe it's not a bad idea. Maybe it's the time for more logic and less folklore."

"Are you joking?," Sybil gasped. "Are you ready to sell out your family's lifeline to a foreign corporation? To a multinational that would probably dilute the wine, bottle it in plastic, and sell it in discount shops around the world?"

Oh, ma chère. n'exagère pas.

"I'm not exaggerating. These people are pirates. I've seen these deals back on Wall Street – hostile takeovers, leveraged buyouts, junk bonds, greenmail. They don't give a damn about the businesses – they just want to make money."

"American firms, yes. But maybe not the Italians. After all, the European Community… "

"European Community, my eye! Everybody's out today for a killing. The Continis are in textiles and banking. What do they know about wine? What do they care?"

"Maybe you're right," Gérard nodded. "But I can still talk to them. It may be amusing."

"I can think of other ways to amuse yourself," Sybil said, though at the moment she couldn't think of one. Why was Gérard so damned complacent?

"Listen," Gérard said, "I'm 62 years old. I have enough money for the rest of my life. I have a nephew who is going to inherit everything, including St.-Cloud. If he wants to sell it someday, I won't be around to tell him what to do. In fact, he's the one who should know about this now. He should be discussing with the Continis, too."

Sybil leaned back on the bench, exasperated. That was exactly what she didn't want – bringing Vincent into it. She closed her eyes and fell silent. Crickets were chirping in the grass, and far away, in the next vineyard, a dog was barking. When she opened her eyes, she saw the moon had risen, and all color was bleached out of it.

"Gérard, maybe I'm being foolish, or sentimental. But I hate to see a place like this turned into a factory. I hate to see something beautiful and unique turned into something ugly and ordinary."

"*Chère Sybil*, you're a wonderful, sensitive woman. And I agree with everything you say. I have spent my whole life making beautiful things – you know that – and I want to do that to my last day. But you know you can't change the world. If you succeed in impressing a few people, changing a few minds, changing a few lives, that is already something. In the end, maybe, you can't even hope for that. You can only hope to keep your own principles, and your own standards, and your own sanity."

"And you feel no obligation to pass that on to others?

To try to enlighten them, or at least educate them? To try to preserve those high standards?"

"Ah, Sybil, you are such an idealist! Such a crusader!"

"Good Lord, Gérard, someone has to stand up for something in this world. You bloody well fought the Germans."

"Of course. Our lives were at stake."

"Not your lives – your *way* of life. Your lives were perfectly safe as long as you obeyed them. But thank God there were some people who wouldn't obey – who realized there's more to life than survival – who were willing to fight for a way of life they believed in –"

"Sybil, enough!"

Gérard was too tired to get into an argument, especially an argument about the war. Sybil fell silent for a few minutes, then she sighed deeply.

"Gérard, I'm sorry. I don't want to pick on you. I only want you to understand what's going on, and urge you to hold on to this place. Maybe I am too emotionally involved with it, but it represents so much to me."

"It means a lot to me, too," Gérard nodded, "and that's why I will talk to these pirates of yours and see what they are proposing. Mutiny? Mutilation? Murder? *Qu'ils fichent le camp.* But if they have a good idea, something that will really help this whole region, maybe I'll go along with them. *Pourquoi pas?*"

It was a reasonable answer and a reasonable attitude, Sybil knew; so why was her stomach still churning? Part of her hoped Gérard was right; part of her prayed he was wrong.

"All right," she said at last. "We'll do it your way. Let's see what they have to offer. But please, promise me I can be with you when you speak to them."

D'accord , Gérard said, sincerely. To him, it was touching to see Sybil's concern. But it was comical, too; he couldn't understand her panic.

The moon was high over the trees now, completely out of grasp; Sybil strained her neck far back to see it. She was limp with fatigue, but she knew she wouldn't sleep well. She decided she would take one of Daniel's Valiums.

"So, we agree and we drink on it? A shot of Calvados to finish the night?", and Gérard rose from his chair.

Sybil rose, too, slowly, and followed him into the pantry.

*   *   *

CHAPTER THREE – *Les Plats*

Sybil downed a second cup of coffee and braced herself for the strenuous morning ahead. It would start with a tour of the neighboring vineyards, visits to some of their cellars, and a pre-lunch wine tasting back at St.-Cloud. A local minibus was ordered for the trip, and while everyone was away, Gérard would have a chance to go marketing and prepare his *boeuf bourguignon*. He and Sybil had decided, back at the beginning of the season, that it was the best dish to serve the guests after they had spent several hours gurgling and gulping red Burgundies. "They'll be stewed just like the meat," Gérard had reasoned.

Sybil considered getting a head start on the day's drinking by adding a splash of Calvados to her coffee – a custom she had discovered in Normandy and found generally repulsive, except on mornings like this – but she realized it was too risky. She could perform her duties being mildly disconsolate; she could not afford to be incoherent.

"My, you're looking grim on this glorious morning. Can I help cheer you up?"

It was Stefano. Of course. Sybil forced a gracious smile and immediately hated herself for it. She wasn't bold enough to say what was on her mind, or turn her back and dramatically walk away, so she just remained silent…. and remained. She hated herself some more.

"It must be very serious indeed if it can't be shared."

She fiddled with her cup, hating him, too.

"Well, may I at least drink my coffee with you and share your silence? I promise not to make any more noise." And he sat down on the stool next to her, crossing his long legs sheathed in those immaculate beige trousers.

Cerruti, she thought. Oh God, I can't sit here dumbly staring at his trousers.

"Would you like a croissant?": an evasive ploy. She started to rise from the stool and he put his hand on her knee.

"Sybil – may I call you Sybil? – I think I know what's on your mind. Daniel has told you about the Contini project and you're very upset. You hate me."

Uncanny, she thought. This man reads minds.

"Tell me – it's true, isn't it?"

"Yes," she said at last, quite relieved that the words had been wrung out of her. "I'm very upset. Regardless what you think, these châteaux are not pizza parlors."

"But my dear lady, of course not. Believe me, this is no fast-food operation. Contini is a very high class company, a conglomerate of top quality industries. If anything, they'll end up improving the product, and the image, and the way of life here."

"Sorry, I'm simply not convinced." His hand was still on her knee, and she squirmed slightly. Why was she feeling so inept, so inarticulate?

His hand moved to her hand that was fidgeting with the cup. "Will you let me try to convince you? Can we have a little chat together this afternoon, after lunch?"

She shook her head. "You can't convince me. I know

this region too well, and the people. Nothing can convince me that bigger is better. Not here, anyway."

"Let me try. Just listen to me once." His voice, with its light accent, was very low, very persuasive. He squeezed her hand gently and smiled.

She smiled back faintly, in spite of herself. Fleetingly, she wished – she imagined – that his interest was something other than business.

"Don't worry," he said, smiling more broadly. "I won't seduce you."

A horn honked outside – it was the bus – and it broke the spell of his voice. Sybil turned to the window with a deliberate nod, and they both rose.

"Off to work," Stefano said gaily.

"Off to work," she echoed.

Everyone was in the courtyard, more or less ready for the outing. Mr. Takashi and Mr. Okura were chattering in Japanese to Patti, helping her load her camera. Stuart was listening, without much interest, to George as he carefully explained why insurance rates were lower in Dallas than in Houston. The Silvers, clad in jogging gear, were doing some warm-ups, while Antoine watched them, incredulously. Sybil trotted up to him.

"That's how Americans stay fit," she said. "Isn't it admirable?"

C'est absurde, replied Antoine.

"Why?," she asked, surprised.

"Because it's artificial. They make the body work for no reason."

"But it's exercise!"

"Exercise! Do you cook a meal for exercise and not eat it? Do you build a house and not live in it?"

"Oh, Antoine – you're such a pragmatist!". Sybil usually enjoyed bantering with him and poking fun at his pig-headedness, but she was not in the mood for it today.

"Come on, let's go see Claude."

Claude, the bus driver, was a tall, muscular man who seemed too big for the vehicle. In fact, he must have felt awkward, because once installed in the driver's seat, he rarely left it, even during the lunch stop. He would eat two *baguettes* slathered with mustard and ham, graciously accept a cup of coffee that Sybil brought him, and puff contentedly on a Gauloise. (Sybil had warned him there would be no tips from Americans if he smoked while driving. Reluctantly, he followed her advice, and only smoked during breaks.)

Salut, mon pote, Antoine waved.

Salut, Claude waved back. *Bonjour, Madame Dickson*.

"Good morning, Claude. All set for the tour?"

Claude nodded good-naturedly. He knew the itinerary by heart, and had almost memorized Sybil's narration. He turned on the ignition and let the engine purr while everyone was rounded up.

Sybil sat alone on a front seat, across from Antoine. Daniel, having made the tour several times, begged off, and Sybil was glad. They had barely spoken to each other since yesterday's discussion. She opened her purse, reapplied some lipstick, and shuffled some papers on her lap. George walked up to her seat and leaned over.

"I hear we're gonna get some free samplings," he grinned.

Sybil looked up. "Yes, there'll be tastings at each place. And a chance to buy the wines you like."

"Sounds like a mighty fine idea," he said, and went to join Helen.

Stefano settled himself across the aisle from Stuart and Patti, the Silvers sat behind him, and the Japanese took the very last seat so they could shoot pictures out the rear window. Claude closed the door and the bus took off: down the private road, onto the main road, and into town.

Following her outline, Sybil pointed out the war memorial, the town hall, and, several miles on, the first cluster of roadsigns that announced the regional wines. The town names read like a newspaper ad, or a fairytale: Nuits-St.-Georges, Vosne-Romanée, Vougeot, Gevrey-Chambertin. This was the northern part of the Côte d'Or, she explained, called the Côtes de Nuits, which produces three-quarters of all the great reds. To the south was the Côte de Beaune, which produces lighter reds and whites.

"As you'll see, these are all small properties, anywhere from one to five acres, one right on top of the other," she explained. "Each one has a slightly different soil and drainage and exposure, which is why each vineyard is called a 'climat'. The great 'climates' in this region face southeast, in order to get the first rays of sun in the morning, which draws up moisture through the plants. And even the slope of the land is important, because that determines the angle at which the sun hits the vines at noon." She paused for breath. "These may seem like trifling details, but each element is important, and affects the final product. That's why, even with the same root stock, you can't reproduce authentic Burgundy wines outside of Burgundy. And the same thing is true of authentic Champagne and authentic Cognac."

George was amazed how small each vineyard was. "Just big enough for a dog-house in Texas," he said.

"Very picturesque, but hardly a cost-efficient way to do business," Stefano said to Stuart, who nodded.

Defiantly, Sybil continued. "The first vines were planted in Burgundy 2500 years ago, but nobody is certain where they came from. Most of the present families have been here for generations. Some of them even have ancestors going back to the Middle Ages, who probably supplied wine to the popes when they were based in Avignon."

"At some point, though, the popes wisely returned to Rome, and cheap Italian Chianti." It was Stefano again. Barbara giggled. She liked his sense of humor.

Sybil swallowed hard. This was going to be a dandy trip.

The bus lurched sharply to the left and turned into a long, dusty driveway. At the end, there was a modest house, some big shade trees, and a dilapidated building farther on – the wine cellar. Everyone left the bus, except Claude. The owner, André Despaille, came running over to shake Sybil's hand, and thumped Antoine on the back.

"It's going well, isn't it?," he chortled. "Good sun, not much rain. We may have a beautiful harvest."

"I'm praying for it," Antoine replied, clasping his hands.

The two men led the group into the dim, dank, limestone cellar, where big oak barrels were lined up against one wall. André spoke almost no English, so Antoine gave the introduction, explaining how the grapes were pressed, and the juice extracted and put through two fermentations. Oak was the traditional and best material for the casks, but at modern plants (they would see one later on), the vats were made of stainless steel.

André's wife arrived with a tray of glasses, as André began opening some bottles. First, they served their five-year old *cru*, then their two-year old wine, and then last year's, which was almost ready to go on the market. Antoine discussed the differences: the fuller body of the older product, the fresh flavor of the younger one. He pointed out the similarities that ran through all of them. Then he demonstrated how to do a proper tasting.

"Three steps," he said. "First, you spin it around in the glass and smell it. No, no – hold the foot of the glass, not the bowl. Inhale slowly. Think what it smells like. Berries? Flowers? Wood?"

Everybody sniffed seriously. Patti sneezed. George raised the glass to his lips.

"No, no!," Antoine barked. "Not yet! Smell it first! Now, take a little in your mouth and put it under your tongue. Keep it there a little while and feel what it tastes like. Maybe sharp? Maybe smooth? Maybe acid? Don't swallow it! Now spit it out."

André passed around a champagne bucket for everyone to spit into.

"What a waste!," George grumbled to Stuart, who noticed with annoyance that a few drops had spilled onto his Lacoste.

"Now," said Antoine, "take a little more into your mouth and keep it in the front, on top of your tongue. Open your lips a little and breathe into your mouth, into the wine."

This was the hardest step for Sybil, and she usually skipped it, although she knew it was important to draw air through the wine to discover its full bouquet, its balance. Daniel could do it perfectly, clamping his teeth like a wildcat and inhaling deeply.

"Now roll it around your tongue," continued Antoine, "and spit it out."

The bucket was passed again.

Finally, Antoine said everyone could take a sip and swallow it. George heaved an audible sigh of relief.

The same process was repeated with all three wines. After each one, Madame Despaille passed around a tray of bread cubes, to clear the palate for the next sample. She herself drank nothing, but André and Antoine seemed to be toasting and drinking nonstop.

Stefano sidled up to Sybil.

"Not bad for a first communion," he whispered. "But I'd like something headier for high mass."

She nearly spluttered out her mouthful. She looked up at him, saw his grin, and grinned back in spite of herself.

"Yes, I'd expect something like that from an Italian. Always mixing up the sacred and the profane!"

"And the spirits and the spiritual," he agreed, clinking

his glass against hers. "To say nothing of oenology and sexology."

Damn, she thought, He was chatting her up again in his charming way. She smiled at him anyway and put down her glass.

"Time to go, I think. On to the next one."

"Signora Dickson, don't you ever let yourself have a good time?" Stefano was still by her side.

"Yes, of course," she said defensively, "but not during working hours."

"But I thought you enjoyed your work."

"I do," she retorted. "And I am. Having a good time. Honestly, you're a terrible tease."

"You're finally starting to appreciate me," he laughed, and poured himself another glass from the five-year old *cru*.

Sybil rounded everyone up and herded them onto the bus, thanked the Despailles, and motioned to Claude to extinguish his cigarette. She was feeling slightly dizzy, and decided she wouldn't do any tasting at the next stop.

*   *   *

The next stop was a good one to miss. The bus pulled into a small parking lot in the village of Chamonet, which seemed to be dominated by a dozen or so wine merchants whose shops were huddled wall to wall. On first sight, they seemed to be competing with each other, but on closer observation it was clear they were comfortably sharing the territory and the trade. Outside, their signs announced 'free wine tastings, no obligation', and once inside, the curious visitor was plied with glass after glass until finally – through sheer exhaustion or intoxication – he purchased a case of something. It was a friendly but deadly soft sell. Sybil discreetly excused herself and took a stroll.

When she returned half an hour later, her guests were in good spirits, hauling cases of Burgundy onto the bus and waving goodbye to the owners. George and Helen were planning a Burgundy barbecue when they returned home, Richard and Barbara decided to have a wine and cheese party, Stuart and Patti were arguing about their guest list, and the Japanese seemed to be worried about import duties. Stefano hadn't bought anything, but looked amused by it all.

Sybil sank into her seat and signaled Claude to drive on.

"Are you feeling all right?," Antoine asked.

She nodded. "Just a little tired."

"Perhaps you should have some coffee at the next stop," suggested Stefano.

"Perhaps I will," she said, surprised at his concern.

During the next several miles, the talking and excitement wound down. The wine was having its effect. It wouldn't matter so much now if everyone was drowsy because the final stop was at a commercial Chablis distillery, where they would be shown 5,000-gallon steel vats and completely automated assembly-line bottling. It was, in a way, a letdown after visiting the private growers, but Sybil felt this was another side of the business and ought to be seen, too. Secretly, she hoped everyone would be thoroughly appalled to see wine being processed like Coca-Cola.

Some of them were. But some of them were impressed:

the Japanese scribbled notes and took pictures.

Antoine found a coffee-dispensing machine near the manager's office and brought Sybil a paper cup of expresso. She drank it gratefully. She checked her watch – it was nearly noon, time to return to St.-Cloud.

As she settled again into her seat, she realized this was the last bus tour for the year. She gazed out the window, at the gentle hills that changed contour at every turn in the road, at the precise stripes of the vineyards, like a corduroy patchwork; at the mossy black slate rooftops, at the pale cerulean sky spotted with a few clouds. She closed her eyes and tried to imprint it in her mind, as if to store it up for the winter months in New York. The image kept slipping away, and she suddenly wished she had a camera.

They were back at St.-Cloud by twelve-thirty. Gérard had prepared a tray of bread and a special bland cheese, made by Trappist monks in nearby Citeaux, and carried it down to the wine cellar. Antoine donned his big sommelier's apron and started opening some bottles. Now he was on home ground, and he became a consummate showman.

As the guests filed in, he handed each one a glass and reminded them of the three steps. Sybil was ready again for some wine; she was hungry, too, and eyed the cheese tray impatiently. The odor of *boeuf bourguignon* wafted faintly down from the kitchen. Heaven above and hell below, she thought. No, this was heaven, too, but with a touch of purgatory. Halfway heaven – like halfway house, like halfway there. She was startled to feel an arm around her shoulder.

"Daydreaming?" It was Daniel. "How was the tour?"

"Just fine," she said.

"No problems with Claude?"

"Not at all. I think he got some nice tips."

"Well, I got a little work done while you were gone." I'll bet, she thought; a few calls to Italy, a fax to New York. "Anything new?" She tried to sound casual, even pleasant.

"No. I sent a fax to New York and made a few calls to Italy. Contini confirmed that his wife is arriving tomorrow."

Sybil shuddered, mentally. How, on the one hand, could a husband of twenty years be such a predictable creature and, on the other hand, be a virtual stranger?

Colette arrived and passed around the cheese. Everyone was enjoying the St.-Cloud wine, as Sybil knew they would. They nibbled and drank until finally. Gérard bellowed from the top of the stairs: *À table!*

*　*　*

By the time lunch was finished it was close to three o'clock. Daniel stood up, stretched, and went over to Gérard and Vincent, who were cleaning up the kitchen, and asked if they'd like to take a walk. They nodded yes – in ten minutes. Mr. Takashi and Mr. Okura went to the salon to look over their notes; Patti and Stuart went to sunbathe on the terrace; the Silvers and the Perkins' went to their rooms for a nap. Sybil went to her office to work for a while on the next day's menus. She was there only a short time when Stefano rapped quietly on the door and walked in.

"What about that little talk you promised me?"

"I didn't promise," said Sybil. "I didn't even say yes."

"Come now! You're an intelligent, open-minded woman. You wouldn't flatly say no to something without hearing all the facts."

"I think I know the facts," she said, averting his eyes.

"Sybil, I have some very important background material, something that just might change your mind. At least take a look at it."

She glanced at him, and he seemed terribly earnest. You're a fool, she said to herself, putting down the stack of menus. "All right," she said to him. "Let's see it."

"Upstairs," he said. "In my room."

Oh God, she thought, that's not very subtle. But he was already taking her by the arm and leading her out. Upstairs, he paused in front of the door to his room.

"Naturally," he said, "you won't tell Daniel I showed this to you. And certainly not in my room!"

"Certainly not!", she mimicked.

He turned the key, and she followed him in. I'm an adult woman, she thought; an adult, married woman. This man can't do anything to me that I don't want him to do. It gave her a little confidence.

Stefano motioned for her to sit down on the couch near the window and he put a small portfolio on her lap. Then, from the oak secretary, he took a bottle of cognac and two snifters. He filled them and handed her one.

"To our friendship," he said.

She said nothing, but accepted the toast. Usually, she

gagged on cognac, so she sipped it very slowly, very carefully. Stefano downed his fast, and poured some more.

"Now," he said, sitting next to her, "here's a prospectus on the Contini group. Just look at this list of affiliates."

She looked. There were banks, retail stores, ready-to wear manufacturers, a construction firm, and yes – a fast-food chain. She pointed that out to him.

"Of course," he said, "but that's not going to have anything to do with wine. Contini is a high-quality conglomerate. St.-Cloud is going to be top-of-the-line, along with the banks and the fashion houses."

She looked at him skeptically.

"Sybil, take all this with you and look it over carefully. When you've read it, we can talk about it again."

"That sounds fair enough," she agreed.

He put his arm around the back of the couch, barely grazing her shoulder.

"I'm really trying to be fair," he said. "You're a very intelligent woman – and a very attractive woman, too – and I'd be an utter fool to try to deceive you."

She couldn't think of anything to say, so she took another sip of cognac, carefully.

"To tell you the truth, I've been a little cowed by you. I'm not used to meeting women like you."

That, she thought, was too obviously a line. She smiled wryly and started to rise. He held her shoulder.

"Don't," he said. "I'm serious."

"I'm sure you've met all kinds of women."

"Yes, I have. But very few like you."

She looked at him quizzically, the avid female wanting to hear more and fearing it.

"You're a very deep person," he went on. "I can tell. You absorb everything. You've got roots in two continents. You're cultured, you're bright, you're good-looking, you're a good wife and mother. You're almost perfect."

Sybil laughed uncomfortably. "So what's missing?"

Stefano brushed a strand of hair off her cheek. "Let's say" – he made it a long pause, a pregnant pause, thought Sybil, which had better abort soon. "Let's say you're a bit uptight."

"Good Lord, if you confuse being civilized with being uptight…."

"My dear Sybil, some of the world's greatest civilizations were most emphatically not uptight. Greek bacchanalia, Roman orgies…."

"Not to mention human sacrifice among the Incas and opium dens in China." He had touched a nerve and she was reacting angrily. "Do you always evaluate people in terms of their emotional extravagance?"

"No," he said quietly. "But it makes me very unhappy to see a lovely woman who is afraid to express her feelings, to face them honestly and explore them completely."

"I'm not afraid," she protested. "I simply prefer to keep them to myself."

"A pity," he said. "I'm sure they're very beautiful." And he kissed her lightly on the cheek. She squirmed, and he put his other arm around her. She found herself stuck, ungracefully, with her arms folded across her lap, and one hand desperately grasping the snifter. Now she couldn't even squirm. He looked into her eyes, and then slowly down her blouse, button by button. When he saw she was clutching the snifter, he quickly took it from her and put it in his other hand, resting on her shoulder. He dipped his finger into the cognac and moistened her lips with it; then he licked it all away.

Oh God, I don't believe this is happening, she thought. Suppose someone walks in? She remembered one evening in New York when she and Daniel had returned home unexpectedly early and found their babysitter half undressed, sandwiched between her boyfriend and the antique Kilim carpet. No, this can't be happening to me.

But Stefano was putting more cognac on her lips, and nibbling them. He put the snifter on the windowsill and pulled her arms around him. They hung limply around his waist; she didn't know what to do; she didn't dare do anything. No matter – he was doing it all. He pulled the Liberty print scarf from her shoulders, and as he unbuttoned her blouse she tried to remember what bra she was wearing: the prim cotton one from Marks and Spencer, or the frilly one from Galeries Lafayette? Good Lord, am I really letting him go that far?

He was going further. Whichever bra it was, he was opening it, then unzipping her skirt. Everything, except her shoes, seemed ready to fall off her. He reached down and slipped off her shoes. At the same time, incredibly, his lips didn't leave hers for a moment.

It's like homecoming weekend at Yale, she thought. It's like that ghastly blind-date I had, before I met Daniel, the boy who wouldn't take his hands off me. It's *adolescent.* But another voice told her it wasn't adolescent at all: that other voice was hissing, "consenting adults".

Suddenly, Stefano stood up and pulled her to her feet. Her skirt fell down to her ankles. He removed her blouse. Her bra was hanging uselessly and he took that off, too. He didn't say a word, but began kissing her neck, her shoulders, her breasts. She trembled, and looked nervously at the door.

"It's locked," he said. "Come." He was pulling her toward the bed.

"No, really."

"Sybil, we're grown-up people."

"You don't understand. I've always been faithful."

"There are different ways to be faithful. The most important thing is to be faithful to yourself." He was kissing her neck again, stroking her back, running his hands though her hair. If she could just sit down and talk to him quietly, and put her clothes back on, she was sure she would be able to salvage herself. But there was no chance – he was mercilessly muffling her resistance.

He nudged her closer to the bed. She stumbled on her skirt, still around her ankles, so he lifted her up and dropped her, a bit clumsily, right onto the flowered spread. She sat there, stunned, as he rapidly pulled off his ascot, removed his shirt, his shoes, his trousers. He had the grace, at least, to leave on his navy blue underpants, and as she still had her underpants on, she felt vaguely protected.

He reached out rapidly and closed the curtain; there was some comfort in that, too. She wanted to see as little as possible; she wanted him to see as little as possible. She felt like a schoolgirl.

He lay down on the bed and drew her next to him. "This is better," he said. In a way it was, in a way it wasn't. She felt less awkward, but much more vulnerable. He was pulling off her underpants.

She tried to wriggle away. "Sybil, Sybil," he said softly. He caressed her. "Let's make this something beautiful." Then his pants came off, too. He rolled on top of her. His chest smelled of musky cologne. Must be Italian, she thought irrelevantly. In any case, it wasn't Aramis, which Daniel wore and which she hated. Oh God, Daniel. Why did she have to think of Daniel now? Stefano was pressing into her, and she forgot Daniel. She tried to remain rigid, to stay controlled, dignified for God's sake. But she found herself moving with him. Her eyes were tightly shut, and wild thoughts flew into the darkness: Anna Karenina, Emma Bovary, fallen women, outraged husbands, duels, private detectives, divorce courts. Like the drowning person seeing his life pass before him, she was watching a lifetime of caution and clichés collide inside her head.

And then, amazingly, it stopped; Stefano was clutching her and heaving. She clung to him as he climaxed; she wasn't even sure of her own climax because she was so absorbed by his.

He settled heavily on top of her, with all his weight. She felt glued to the bedspread, and dizzy, and dazed. Minutes passed, and finally he murmured "*bellissimo*", and rolled off her, keeping one arm flung across her chest. With his other arm he reached for the cigarettes on the night-table and a gold lighter. As he lit up, she pulled a corner of the rumpled bedspread over herself, and examined him out of the corner of her eyes: fairly broad shoulders, long arms that must have been powerful at one time, a slight thickening around the torso but no flab. She skipped nervously over the pelvis. Nice legs, long narrow feet. It was an older body than Daniel's (she startled herself at the comparison, but after all, whom else could she compare him to?), and less well cared for, but attractive nonetheless.

"Why are you staring at me?," he smiled, exhaling deeply.

"I'm not staring at you," she lied, surprised that he had noticed.

"It's all right if you do. There are just the normal signs of wear and tear."

"I'd say you're quite well preserved for your age."

He pretended to wince. "How tactless of you!"

She laughed. She was starting to relax now. What was that ridiculous Latin expression about sadness after coitus? She was feeling unaccountably well.

"Haven't you ever been married?," she asked, just as unaccountably.

"Never," he said.

"Why not?" She could think of a dozen reasons, actually, but was eager to hear his answer.

"Do you really think I'm the kind of man who would enjoy being married?"

"That would depend a lot on the woman you married."

"That's placing far too much responsibility on a woman. My own sense of responsibility being rather limited, I think I did the world a favor staying single. Undoubtedly. I've made many more women happy that way."

Sybil hated his conceit. "You're bragging." she said.

"No. I'm being honest. Married, I would have made countless women unhappy and one woman utterly miserable. Single, I'm nobody's heartache."

"I'm sure you've broken many hearts along the way." But mine isn't going to be one of them, she added to herself.

"Ah, you flatter me," he said, stroking her cheek a bit absentmindedly, with the back of his free hand.

"No, that's not my intent. If anything, I was criticizing you." She sounded peevish, she knew, but suddenly, she saw herself as one among hundreds of women, "his" women. She detested all of them, she detested him, she detested herself for being in this situation. She pulled the free edge of the bedspread more tightly around her and wondered if she could possibly get off the bed and into her clothes while keeping her body covered. Not unless Stefano got off the spread first.

No chance of that. He lit another cigarette and snuggled close to her.

"And what about you? Why did you give it all up and get married?"

"I didn't give anything up," she said, again on the defensive. "I was twenty years old and in love and it was the normal thing to do."

"And it still seems normal to you?"

"Yes, of course."

He took a deep, silent drag on the cigarette, flicked the ashes, and looked up at the ceiling. "Maybe the problem is that I'm too much of an idealist."

"What do you mean?"

"Part of me has always believed in perfect, lasting love, and another part of me says bullshit, there's no such thing. Unfortunately, my personal experience has borne out the second thesis."

Was this a line? Was she falling for it? With more hope than conviction she said, "Maybe you never really gave the first thesis a fair try."

"Maybe I never met the right woman."

He's saying everything I want to hear, she thought, quite lucidly. Then, quite stupidly, she kissed his shoulder. "I really must get dressed and get out of here."

He held her back. "Sybil, I admire you tremendously. And after what has just happened between us, there's a great deal more than admiration." He kissed the palm of her hand. "I do want to see you again, and soon, and often."

She started to protest, of course, politely, but he went on. "Believe me, I don't go around breaking up marriages or jeopardizing my business relationships for a fast roll in the hay. In fact, it's going to be just as hard for me to face Daniel as it will be for you."

She shuddered: he has uttered the unmentionable.

"Stefano, this must never, never be found out."

"Of course not. It would be as awkward for me as for you."

Awkward, she thought frantically, was a monumental understatement.

"It will be our secret," he said reassuringly. But she wasn't reassured. She fidgeted with the fringe on the bedspread. "Trust me," he said, "and I'll trust you."

She was completely confused now; her head was spinning. Marriages and mergers, adultery and acquisitions, bedrooms and boardrooms. How did she get into this mess?

"Please, I've got to go."

"In a moment." He kissed her passionately, but with a strong flavor of tobacco. She overlooked it.

"May I have the bedspread?" He pulled it out from under him and she nervously wrapped it around herself before getting up, grabbing her clothes, and running into the bathroom. She didn't look in the mirror. She washed superficially, knowing she would shower in her own bathroom and put on fresh clothes.

Her hair was a mess, but she didn't dare use his hairbrush – it seemed too intimate. Intimate? You've just had sex with the man! She couldn't explain her reaction; she never used Daniel's hairbrush, either.

Stefano was tying on a black kimono when she came out. He looked calm and refreshed.

"Sybil," he said, putting his arms around her. She let him hold her for a few seconds, as if to draw some strength to walk out the door. Should she look through the keyhole first, to make sure no one was in the hall? Perhaps he could open it a crack, and look himself. This was starting to resemble a *comédie de boulevard*.

"Will you make sure no one is outside?," she asked.

He looked. "The coast is clear!," he chuckled.

"Please, this isn't funny." She felt like a thief. He kissed her once again as she slipped out the door.

*   *   *

Daniel put on his sunglasses, but the mid-afternoon glare didn't bother Gérard and Vincent. They walked slowly between the impeccable rows of vines. "How does it look to you?," Daniel asked, as Gérard stopped to examine some of the hard, green grapes.

"Not bad," he said. "Not bad at all. If we say our prayers every night, it may be a good harvest."

Daniel decided it was time to broach the question. "Don't you ever get tired of this, year after year?"

"It's my life," Gérard shrugged. *N'est-ce pas, Vincent?*

"Of course," agreed Vincent, brushing away a fly.

"But it's tough work. You live under pressure for eight months a year, and you're never sure from one year to the next what the results will be."

"*Mais, c'est la vie.* You work under pressure, too, don't you, and you never know what the results will be." Gérard was checking the underside of some leaves now, making sure there was no mildew.

"Well, it's different in an office. There are other people to share the responsibilities and the risks."

"You think I need some partners?" Gérard stood up, and looked directly into Daniel's Ray-Bans. What was the

English expression? 'Beating around the bush.' Enough bush-beating!

Daniel wasn't prepared for that kind of abrupt reaction, and he cleared his throat. "Well, yes, it may be something for you to consider."

Gérard smiled slyly. "Alright, I'm considering. What do you have to offer?"

This is really absurd, thought Daniel. What does he know? What has Sybil told him?

"Well," he said, "I personally have nothing to offer, but I've been in contact with a major Italian group that has expressed some interest in St.-Cloud."

"How much?," asked Gérard

"How much?," gulped Daniel. Gérard seemed ready to sign on the dotted line.

"How much interest?," Gérard asked.

"Well, a great deal of interest, if they can purchase enough property in the region to make it worthwhile. Actually, they're approaching you first because of your reputation. For food as well as wine. They're hoping that once you see what a good idea it is, you might swing the others."

Gérard scratched his head and looked off into the distance. "What do you think, Vincent? Are we ready to turn this into Castello Santa-Cloud?"

Daniel could't tell if Gérard was being sarcastic or serious. Vincent took a while to answer. "I don't know," he said finally. "It's something to think about."

"I know they're prepared to make a good deal with

you," said Daniel. "Naturally, they'll want to keep Vincent, and they'll bring in the best experts in Europe to run the business. Real professionals." No, that sounded like a slur on Gérard. "Professional managers, I mean."

"Ah, *managers*," said Gérard, with an exaggerated French accent.

The three men were silent for a while. Then Vincent asked, "When can we meet these buyers?"

"Well, you'll have the pleasure of meeting Mrs. Contini tomorrow," Daniel replied. "She's the wife of the chairman of the board. But for actual negotiations, Stefano di Carozza is your man. He's Contini's personal assistant."

Vincent looked surprised.

"You understand now," said Gérard. "He's not here for cooking lessons."

"Did you already know about this, *tonton*?," asked Vincent.

Gérard didn't answer. He walked a few yards down the row, turned around, and came back. He faced Daniel squarely.

"I want to know how much they are offering for the château, who is going to manage it, whether they will keep the *appellation contrôlée*, and what my position will be."

"Fine," said Daniel. "Then let's set up a meeting for tomorrow evening, after dinner."

"And Vincent, too," Gérard added. "St.-Cloud is his inheritance, so his opinion must also be heard."

"Absolutely," agreed Daniel, glad that Gérard had suggested it before he did. He held out his hand to shake on the agreement, but Gérard waved it away.

"Nothing yet – nothing. We are just agreeing to talk."

"That's a start," said Daniel, "and a very good one."

*   *   *

Vincent hurried into the kitchen behind Gérard.

"It's incredible, no? To think they picked St.-Cloud as their first choice!"

"As their first target," Gérard said sternly.

"Don't you like the idea?"

"*Ecoute, fiston.* In the old days, there were generals and infantry. Today, there are bankers and businessmen. The battle is the same. *La guerre n'est pas finie.*"

"But if they can really modernize the business, make it more cost-efficient, increase the overall production."

"And lower the quality." Gérard began getting some ingredients together for the afternoon demonstration of *barbue au beurre blanc.*

Vincent sighed. "You've already thought about this and you've made up your mind."

"I've made up three-quarters of my mind," Gérard admitted. "The last quarter is open to discussion. Maybe Madame Contini, if she's very charming, will be able to convince me there are fantastic advantages."

Vincent knew that flippant tone; it meant his uncle was prevaricating. It was time to talk straight.

"One advantage would be securing my own future," he said. "It would be much more stable to be part of an international group."

"You think so?"

"Of course. More money, more resources, a broader base, a bigger market. "

"Bigger problems," said Gérard. "More headaches."

"Uncle, you have a very limited view. You're talking now like a *petit provincial*."

"That's exactly what I am," Gérard answered angrily. "And you're the son of one."

"Yes, God help me." Vincent slammed down a saucepan and stormed out to the terrace. Gérard continued peeling and chopping shallots. He was used to his nephew's temper, but he was sorry that the outburst this time was over the future of St.-Cloud. In fact, it was over the future, period. Gérard often joked about his own mortality, but he hated to think, specifically, of a time when he might not be around to run things. It was *impensable*. It reminded him of funerals and churches. Irritably, he rinsed his hands and adjusted his toque. Later, when Vincent calmed down, they would have to talk things over.

It was nearly four o'clock, and some of the guests began to arrive for the demonstration. Sybil was late; usually, she made sure to be there a few minutes early. Vincent came back in from the garden, quiet but clearly sulking. When Sybil did walk in, she seemed nervous. Daniel must have told her about our talk, thought Gérard. *Merde.* Money destroys more marriages than sex.

* * *

It had been another excellent meal: *tête de veau vinaigrette, barbue au beurre blanc*, a selection of cheeses, and raspberry sorbet. Vincent, still sulking, excused himself after the preparation and drove into town, so that made thirteen at the table. Antoine offered to eat at the counter, but Sybil insisted he pull up a chair and join them. She made sure to place as many people as possible between herself and Stefano. He ended up sitting between Barbara and Helen, and chatted cheerfully to both of them – especially to Barbara, Sybil noticed. But each time she looked at him, ever so furtively, he caught her glance and returned it with a smile. She prayed it wasn't as obvious to the others as it was to her.

She led her contented little band into the salon for coffee. Colette set out the silver service, the expresso cups, and a dish of chocolate truffles. Daniel went over to the stereo and pulled out a few cassettes. Patti and Stuart stretched out on one sofa, and Helen and George settled into the other one. Mr. Takashi and Mr. Okura politely asked each couple if they might join them. Barbara and Richard sat in the two armchairs near the window, watching the sky darken. Stefano stood near the fireplace, leaning against the bookshelves. When Sybil handed him his coffee, he smiled at her again, and his hand grazed hers on the saucer. The cup rattled. To her, it sounded like a kettledrum.

This was History Night – the evening when she told her guests about Burgundy, about its turbulent past, about the Burgundian dukes and their fabulous exploits, the religious wars, Charles VII and Joan of Arc. Gérard and Antoine, finished in the kitchen, slipped in while she was reciting and poured themselves some coffee. Daniel, appropriately, put on a recording of French medieval music, and placed a bottle of Armagnac on the coffee table. It was his private little joke, ever since his wine merchant in New York told him the Armagnacs and the Burgundians were once bitter rivals.

Sybil used notes and charts while she spoke, for it was hard to keep all the names and lineage straight – too many Philippes, for one thing, and a tangle of marriages among all the royal houses of Europe.

"They were marriages of convenience," said Stefano at one point, "like most marriages today. Only then it was for power and sovereignty. Today it's merely for money or sentiment."

"I think sentiment is a good reason," said Barbara dreamily.

"It's less convenient than money," said Stefano.

"Money *and* sentiment is the best combination," said Stuart, staring at the ceiling. Patti poked him playfully in the ribs.

"Yes, but that's rare," mused Stefano. "Probably, we should simply go back to the old ways, to cold-blooded matrimony and socially significant alliances."

"What about people who have no social significance?," queried Daniel, enjoying the banter.

Stefano smiled broadly. "They will have the dubious privilege of marrying for love."

Sybil felt ill. After making love with her that very afternoon, how could he say these things? She tried to get back to the sixteenth century.

"Well, here's a good love story for you – Henri II and Diane de Poitiers. He adored her, and decorated his palaces with their combined initials, like this." She held up a heavy art book with a picture of the interlaced H and D.

"Much to the chagrin of his Italian wife, Catherine de Medici," added Stefano.

Sybil glared at him. Daniel handed him a glass of Armagnac, laughing. "I'm surprised an Italian mamma would let her frog prince get away with that."

"Well, it was another example of the fortuitous separation of love and marriage," replied Stefano, "which is certainly just as desirable as the separation of church and state. Although that took much longer to achieve." He sipped his Armagnac contentedly.

George, who had been thumbing through one of the history books, suddenly exclaimed, "Gol-Iy! Those folks sure didn't live long. Look here – 57 years old, 46 years old, 38 years old."

"Henri II died at forty. He was jousting in a tournament and got a lance through his eye." It was Daniel, sharing one of his favorite bits of historical trivia.

"Must have been a horrible death," said Richard. "Right through the optic nerve into the brain."

"Please," said Barbara weakly, "spare us the details."

"At least it would have been fast," mused Richard, absorbed by the medical possibilities. "With a wound like that, he couldn't have lasted more than a few hours."

Barbara rose from her chair and poured herself an Armagnac. "There is something macabre about the medical profession," she sighed. "Richard adores performing these mental autopsies – he just does it automatically. I really must apologize to you all – it's hardly appropriate after- dinner conversation." She poured Richard an Armagnac, too, to take his mind off the eye.

"Well, I'm relieved to know it was a fast death," said Daniel, not minding the conversation at all.

"Imagine how it would be if it happened today," said Stefano. "He'd be rushed to the hospital, given a transfusion en route, then have his eye removed, then undergo major brain surgery, and finally be put on a life support system in an intensive care ward for the rest of his life – which could be weeks or months or years. Assuming he didn't fall into a coma, his entire court would be transferred to the hospital, daily medical reports would be issued to the press, and Diane and Catherine would have a tearful reconciliation by his bedside. What a fantastic media event!"

Richard was silent; he was not going to let this clown pull him into another discussion of medical ethics. Barbara watched him and held her breath. Sybil, fortunately, had the wits to break the spell.

"Then perhaps it was just as well he died fast, on the field of glory."

Stefano looked at her, almost tenderly. "Yes," he agreed, "some agonies shouldn't be prolonged. Anyway, where would all our religions be if suffering saints and martyrs were simply sedated, operated on, and nursed back to health?"

"Well," ventured Barbara, "a lot of those Bible stories are inspirational."

"Nonsense. It's sheer hypocrisy," Stefano shot back. "And boring besides. Look, we all know enough about human psychology to know that whatever we suppress is the very thing that obsesses us. For the Americans, at least until the 'sixties, the big taboo was sex."

"And now?," queried Barbara.

"Why, it's death. Mortality. Your husband knows that."

Richard didn't say a word. Stefano continued. "The British obsession is money. The Italian obsession is power. The Scandinavian obsession is security. Whatever people feel deficient or impotent or guilty about, that's what they avoid discussing."

"Yes, it makes sense," admitted Daniel, "but you're just talking about western culture now. I don't know if it holds true for the middle east, or the far east, or even for eastern and central Europe."

"Of course it does," said Stefano. "The Arab taboo, their obsession, is love. The Indian obsession is discipline. The Chinese obsession is freedom. The Japanese obsession, if you'll excuse me," he said, bowing to the Japanese, who didn't seem to be following his thesis, "is pride. Self-esteem. As far as eastern and central Europe, or even the Soviet Union, God alone knows what hang-ups they're going to pull out of the bag."

"Well, whatever they are, they'll be better than what they had," said Richard.

"Not necessarily," said Stefano. "They've just come out of a long slumber, which of course to our eyes looks like a nightmare. But you know the hardest part of a nightmare is waking up, and getting your grip on reality again."

"Those Communists have got a helluva lot of catching up to do," interrupted George. "And I'm not so sure we oughta help them."

Daniel hated that kind of myopic attitude. "Look," he said, "they've lost and they know it. Capitalism has won, and by helping them now, we're not only doing them a favor but we're doing ourselves a favor. There are enormous markets to be tapped out there."

Suddenly, Stefano looked exasperated. "Just a moment. Capitalism hasn't won a thing, except maybe by default. You Americans are the biggest debtor country in the world. You're losing ground every day to Japan, and in two years you're going to be locked out of Europe. This time around, it's America that will need a Marshall Plan."

Sybil agreed with him, but she didn't want to come out against Daniel. "Well, at least," she said, "we have a more peaceful world now."

"Mrs. Dickson," Stefano intoned, and she cringed at his public formality, "I wish I could agree with you. But just look at the world right now. Every region, every ethnic group, every little tribe wants its autonomy. We have evolved from the 'Me' generation to the 'We' generation, but it's a very petty 'We'. There is no sense of nationhood, no unifying ideals or ideology, and so everybody scraps with everybody else in the name of independence. It's on a smaller scale, but it's still war."

The music had stopped. Daniel went to the tapedeck and put on some German Lieder. The singing seemed to lift the mood a bit.

"So, what's on for tomorrow?," Barbara asked cheerfully. Sybil, strangely muted by Stefano's words, pulled out her agenda and menus. "Well, the morning class will cover three classics: *salade niçoise, blanquette de veau*, and puff pastry. In the afternoon demonstration, Gérard will prepare marinated salmon and a duck pâté, which actually will be saved for Thursday's meals, since tomorrow night we're scheduled to eat out. We'll be going to a local two-star restaurant, La Cloche d'Or."

"It's the cook's night off," smiled Daniel, handing Gérard and Antoine a glass of Armagnac. They smiled back, raising their glasses.

A hush fell over the room, a kind of contentment that snuffed out the discussion. Mr. Takashi and Mr. Okura had stopped scribbling notes; Helen and George were nodding sleepily; Barbara and Richard, limp in their armchairs, were holding hands; Stuart had his arm around Patti; Daniel was at the window, quietly looking out; Sybil had her eyes closed, listening to the music; Stefano was still standing, leaning against the bookcase, humming softly. *Nach Frankreich zogen zwei Grenadier', die waren in Russland gefangen.*

He had a low, rich voice. Gérard, standing on the other side of the room with Antoine, couldn't understand a thing, neither Fischer-Dieskau nor Stefano di Carozza – but he was pleasantly lulled.

Suddenly, he jolted. A particle of a memory had zipped through his brain. What was this flash of *déjà vu*? What in God's name was he remembering? He stood there, his mouth open, waiting for some image to form.

"Antoine," he whispered, "come with me."

Qu'est-ce qu'il y a?, murmured Antoine.

Viens, he insisted.

The two men tiptoed out, to the pantry.

"I tell you, it's unbelievable," whispered Gérard.

"What is?," said Antoine, perplexed.

"That singing, that voice. That German. I could swear it's Stefan Durschmidt."

Antoine looked at him, incredulous.

"Carozza? But you're mad. He's Italian. And Durschmidt would never dare come back to Lacelle."

"I wouldn't think so. But you know what nerve he had. And with a new name, a new identity… "

Antoine fell silent, trying to superimpose this stranger's face on the old, familiar face: Stefan, the Austrian boy, their friend, who came to Lacelle every summer with his parents, the owners of the Auberge Bleu Danube.

"He wouldn't dare come back here," Antoine repeated, starting to see the resemblance.

"If he felt safe enough, he would," said Gérard.

"How can we know for sure?"

"Let me take care of it," said Gérard. "I'll make an investigation."

"It can't be Stefan," Antoine insisted. "The bastard! *Le salaud.*"

*   *   *

Chapter Four - *Entre Poire et Fromage*

A light rain was falling Wednesday morning, enough to dampen everyone's spirits. Antoine was happy about it, though: he said the vines needed it.

Sybil had slept badly. Still tossing at two in the morning, she had gone to the medicine cabinet to take one of Daniel's Valiums – something she hated to do and rarely did. Daniel had stirred when she returned to bed.

"Any problem?," he mumbled.

"No, just a little restless," she had answered. Restless in the head, she thought. Gnawed by a guilty conscience, poisoned by forbidden fruit. Wondering, in spite of herself, if the brief excitement she had felt with Stefano could rightfully be called passion; wondering if he would approach her again; wondering what she would do if he did.

And besides all that, she had this queer sense of exposure, of being naked in the world – the way she felt after she and Daniel had scrambled into bed and made love for the first time. Ages ago – it was commencement weekend at Yale. Daniel's parents were lunching with the dean, and his roommate was shopping for beer. His cap and gown were hanging on the door, like an observer. It was her first experience, it was fast, it was furtive, it was frantic. And Sybil was reminded of it every time she heard "Pomp and Circumstance".

She gathered up her menus and recipes for the day and went to the kitchen. Gérard was conferring with Colette; he glanced up when Sybil entered and came over.

Bonjour, Sybil – *ça va?*

Ça va, she lied.

"A little rain to cool things off."

Indeed, she thought.

"Vincent didn't like the strawberries in the market today, so we've decided to make the charlotte with pears instead," he continued.

"That's fine," she said. "I'll change it on the menus." Oh, if only all the questions in life could be reduced to pears or strawberries. She went through the menus, one by one, drew a line through *"fraise"* and printed in *"poire"*.

The guests were lingering over their coffee. Sybil gave them, and herself, a few extra minutes before calling them into the kitchen. Barbara and Richard were cheerful and wide awake, but the others seemed sluggish. Stefano, as usual, was late. When he finally appeared – Gérard was already assembling the charlotte – he had an absent-minded air about him. He greeted Sybil without any particular emotion. Exactly as it should be, she thought, but she was disappointed.

The main course was to be *goujonettes de sole* – a deceptively simple dish that required careful slicing of the fish into narrow strips, followed by perfect deep-frying. Gérard showed the class how to dry the strips and roll them, ever so lightly, in flour. He tested the heat of the oil by dropping a cube of bread into it, and seeing how fast it browned.

"More accurate than a thermostat," said Sybil. Helen was shaking her head incredulously.

"If he used an electric deep-fryer, there wouldn't be any problem at all," she said.

Sybil blithely ignored the remark, and continued to discuss how Gérard had prepared the first course, the pâté, the day before. She explained that all meat pâtés improved in flavor if they were allowed to stand for twenty-four hours; this allowed the juices to settle and the flavors to blend. Fish pâtés were different: they were better eaten fresh, the same day they were made. This is ridiculous, she thought. My mind's a million miles away. No, not quite – it's right over there. She shot a quick glance at Stefano, who was gazing out the window, toward the courtyard. He's bored, she thought; not even amused, just bored. Is he wondering how to get me into bed again? Or is he thinking about the Contini takeover bid? Oh, Lord – she suddenly remembered that the Contini woman was arriving today. Maybe he's thinking about that, about her. Maybe he wants to get *her* into bed. Maybe he already has.

" ...on a bed of rice." It was Barbara reading aloud the recipe. Sybil dragged her mind back to the group.

"Yes, the *goujonettes* are very good with rice for a main course. But they can also be served alone, just a small quantity, as a first course."

How was she going to get through the week?, Sybil wondered. Here she was, warning Gérard not to sell out to the satanic scheme and hating Daniel for his involvement in it, and she herself slept with the devil.

A shudder seized her: might Stefano try blackmail? Would he threaten to tell Daniel about their episode if she didn't support the takeover plan?

Someone nudged her; it was Daniel. "Hey, Syb, you're daydreaming."

No, nightmaring. "Sorry," she said, "I was just thinking I had to call La Cloche d'Or"

She excused herself on this flimsy pretext and hurried to her office, dialed the number, and asked for Monsieur Jean, the owner.

Bonjour, Madame, he boomed, with a slight roll to his R. He was from Marseille. Nevertheless, he had all but forsaken the cuisine of the Midi – the garlic and olive oil and tomatoes – and he received his two stars for true Burgundian cooking.

Sybil tried to greet him just as cheerfully. She confirmed that there would be fifteen for dinner that evening, and she went over the menu with him. The wines would be his own selection. Everything was in order. She thanked him and hung up. She turned to leave, and there was Stefano standing at the door.

"*Bonjour,* Sybil," he smiled.

"Hello," she gasped. "What can I, do for you?"

"What a question!," he laughed, and kissed her lightly on the cheek.

"Please," she pleaded, "there are people around."

"No, everybody is in the kitchen frying fish."

"Stefano," – it was strange to call him that –

"Yes, Sybil?" Was he mocking her?

"Look, I don't know what happened to me yesterday. It shouldn't have happened. I feel dreadful about it."

"Really? I'm feeling quite well, actually. I had hoped you'd be feeling very well, too."

His tone was maddening. She wished that someone

would come barging in. Or that the phone would ring. How do you talk to a man you've just slept with and barely know?

The phone did ring. It was Monsieur Jean calling back to ask if she wanted the *apéritif* served in the lounge or at the table. In the lounge, she thought, and said, *à ce soir*.

Stefano put his arm on her shoulder as she put down the phone.

"You're a marvelous administrator," he said.

"It's not so hard," she said, embarrassed by the compliment.

"If Contini does buy the château, I would certainly recommend that they retain you."

His words struck her like bricks. So, he was bargaining after all. She snapped angrily, "If Contini buys the château, you may be sure I won't be bought with it."

"Sybil, please listen to me."

"I must get back to the kitchen."

"You haven't even read the material I gave you."

She looked at him, having forgotten all about it. "You left it in my room."

At least, she thought miserably, she had left that and not a pair of panties.

"I really must get back."

He was standing at the door again, but he slowly moved aside and let her pass.

"We'll talk later," he said, invitingly.

She hurried into the kitchen, nodded to Gérard, examined the fish, and said – in a voice that was inexplicably prim – "Well, then. let's have our *apéritif*."

* * *

Sybil left right after lunch to run some errands in town: pick up fresh flowers at the *fleuriste,* order some brioches for tomorrow's breakfast. It was a nuisance going out in the drizzle, but she needed an excuse – any excuse – to get away from the château for a while. Stefano had adroitly slipped into a chair next to her at lunch, and although he didn't say one direct word to her throughout the meal, his leg pressed constantly against her own. He tried to catch her as she hurried out to the car, saying he wanted to give her "the material".

"Later," she said, and fled.

She spent more time than necessary chatting with the baker and the florist. Then she killed another quarter of an hour at the *pharmacie,* picking out some herbal teas and a can of hairspray. She arrived back at St.-Cloud just in time to hand over the flowers to Colette and join the demonstration class.

Today, Gérard was going to explain the complicated, correct and infallible way to make *feuilleté* pastry. Sybil knew this by heart: cutting in the cold butter, chilling the pastry for an hour, rapidly rolling it out, folding it four times, chilling it again, and repeating the rolling and folding operation yet once more before it was finally ready to use. The result was invariably a feathery, flaky confection that had no equal in the world, but the tedious preparation was simply uninspiring to her. It wasn't anything like the magic chemistry of making a perfect soufflé, or even the delicious anticipation of baking bread and nervously watching the dough rise. *Feuilleté*, she thought, is the pits of haute cuisine.

Still, Gérard didn't seem to mind the drudgery. He was going to use the pastry to make a delectable first course for dinner – *asperges en feuilleté*. As the French asparagus season was over, Vincent had reluctantly bought some Spanish asparagus that morning. Having just switched from strawberries to pears, he realized he couldn't take another liberty with the menu. It didn't make much difference to Gérard. "By the time we get finished with them," he said, "they'll lose their Spanish accent."

And indeed, he subjected those Iberian stalks to some rough treatment: thorough rinsing and scrubbing of the heads, heartless cutting and paring of the stems, parboiling just long enough to make them lose their snap but keep their color. The brief cooking was the equivalent of "al dente" for Italian pasta, Sybil explained – keeping a food's crispness – and it was especially important when cooking vegetables.

At this point, she launched into one of her favorite soliloquies about English cuisine, and its strange obsession for water-logged legumes. As a food writer, she had crusaded against this for years, but still found soggy turnips sliding around her dinner plate in London.

"That's what happens when a civilization outlives its time," chortled Stefano.

"Pardon?," said Sybil.

"It's a kind of ancient regime paranoia. Fear of foul play. Fear of extinction. Thus, an exaggerated cautiousness concerning anything new or natural. A tunnel to France, for example, is seen as an invitation to invasion, and an undercooked turnip is regarded as a seething bed of germs."

How very amusing, thought Sybil, but she was always annoyed when someone else criticized the British. She rose to their defense.

"I do think you're unfair. The British have been very innovative in certain fields, and if they opposed the Channel tunnel all these years, up until now, it's with good cause. We've been attacked often enough by foreign powers. We really don't need to build a royal road for them."

"That was in the past," replied Stefano. "These days, there really isn't much left in old England that anyone would want to go after. Frankly, the main threat of a tunnel is that it will allow too many of Her Majesty's subjects to escape, quickly and cheaply."

"And spend debauched weekends in Paris," laughed Daniel, enjoying Stefano's humor.

"Exactly," said Stefano, "assuming they were willing to take the risk of eating undercooked turnips."

Sybil was exasperated, and on the verge of being angry. It seemed both Daniel and Stefano were making fun of her. Luckily, Gérard had reached the last, critical phase with the *feuilleté* and needed her help to explain the next step.

In fact, Sybil noted, Gérard seemed a bit preoccupied, more quiet than usual. Wasn't he feeling well? He had excused himself at lunch after barely tasting the first course. Odd. She would speak to him later.

* * *

The demonstration session had just ended, and the guests were going to their rooms to change for dinner, when a white car streaked into the courtyard and screeched to a halt.

There were three short blasts on the horn, a door opened and slammed shut, and Sybil – from the large kitchen window – saw a woman standing there, hands on her hips, a cigarette dangling from her mouth. She was wearing a white sweater and pants, yards of gold chains, enormous black sun-goggles, and her blond-streaked hair was tied back with a scarf.

Daniel and Stefano, still in the kitchen, came over to look, too, and Stefano exclaimed, "Lucinda!", and ran outside.

"Well, I guess that's Mrs. Contini," said Daniel, eyeing her. "Not bad."

"She's fifty, if she's a day," said Sybil, piqued at Stefano's alacrity and Daniel's interest.

"Of course," said Daniel, "but she's very well turned out. A lot of class."

"A lot of money." Sybil didn't like her already.

She was putting one arm around Stefano's neck as he bent down to kiss her – amicably, not passionately, Sybil noted – two times on both cheeks, Italian style. They exchanged a few words and then he turned toward the château with a sweeping gesture. She looked at it, studied it from behind her dark glasses, and nodded ever so slightly. Then, abruptly, she strode back to the Alfa Romeo and had Stefano lift out her two bags.

Vuitton, of course, thought Sybil. "I'd better go meet her," she said to Daniel, untying her apron and running her hand through her hair. Pity she didn't have time to change her clothes and spray on a little perfume.

They were just inside the front door when she arrived.

"Mrs. Dickson, I'd like you to meet Mrs. Contini," said Stefano, in a most formal tone of voice.

The women exchanged "how do you do's" and shook hands, just as formally.

"Did you have a pleasant drive?," Sybil asked, as if she cared.

"Rather boring in terms of scenery. And you can't make any time on these local roads. They're jammed with farm trucks."

"Mrs. Contini likes fast autoroute driving," Stefano explained, needlessly.

"Darling, I didn't buy a sports car to play kiddie-car," she retorted, with a sardonic smile.

Sybil lurched when she heard "darling". Was she one of those women who use the term with everyone, from the maid to the lover, or was there a special relationship between her and Stefano after all? And if there was, why should she care? She swallowed hard, and suggested that Mrs. Contini might like to see her room and freshen up. Yes, she would. Sybil called for Colette.

"Well, that's the boss's wife," Stefano said, after she went upstairs. "A bit abrasive, but a heart of 18-karat gold."

"I can imagine," Sybil said dourly. "Why hasn't her husband come?"

"He's in New York at the moment, working on another deal. Anyway, he felt the Burgundy venture was more a woman's domain – a prestige product, cultural implications, you know – and he trusts his wife's taste."

That's probably all he can trust in her, thought Sybil, surprised at her own sudden cattiness.

"She's American, isn't she?"

"Yes, straight out of the pits of Pittsburgh."

"They say you can take the girl out of Pittsburgh but you can't take Pittsburgh out of the girl. To paraphrase what they say about boys from Brooklyn, I mean." Where, she wondered, was this boldness coming from?

"And what about girls from London?," Stefano purred, leaning over her.

"I daresay it's also true," she admitted. And she was pleased, outstripping him on this one. London was certainly a better place to carry around all one's life than Pittsburgh.

"Well, if you'll excuse me, Sybil, I think I'd better change for dinner. This Cloche d'Or place – is it a formal place?"

"Not at all. It's just the local gentry, plus now and then a few Parisians out slumming in the provinces. With their Michelin Guide, of course."

"Of course. Then I guess I fall into the second category and will have to wear a blazer, rather than my workaday overalls. *Ciao*."

He winked, and went upstairs.

*   *   *

Stefano knocked on the door and walked right in. Lucinda had changed into a black negligée and was hanging up some clothes.

"These damn armoires are such a nuisance," she said. "When are the French going to discover walk-in closets?"

"Probably not until they discover Jacuzzis and microwave ovens," Stefano replied, stretching out on the bed.

"It's like visiting the Third World," Lucinda called from the bathroom. "Look at the size of this wash basin. And there's no make-up mirror, no hair dryer..."

"You can borrow mine," Stefano offered. "Free of charge."

"You are a generous dear," Lucinda smiled, re-emerging from the bathroom and walking over to the bed. She lit a cigarette and stood over him, still smiling. "How are things going?"

"Not too badly. I still have to sit down with Bordet and his nephew and give them a good sales pitch. But that will be easier now that I've worked out most of the financial details with Dickson. He's top-notch. His wife, though, is very sentimental about this place, and she's Bordet's confidante. She sees winemaking as a kind of holy art, and Burgundy as the last bastion of Western civilization."

"Surely you can change her ideas about that. Wouldn't she yield to a little bakchich?"

"I'm afraid she's not the type. Unlike you, my dear." He pulled her down on top of him.

"You seem to have gotten to know her fairly well, in

such a short time." She blew a cloud of smoke in his face.

"All in the line of duty," Stefano said, waving away the smoke.

"*What* in the line of duty?," she asked, only half jesting.

"Oh, come now. You're just flattering me, pretending to be jealous."

"Stefano, I know you. There are two things in the world you can't resist – an attractive woman and an attractive deal."

"Oh, Sybil's not my type."

"'*Sybil!* Goddam it, you *have* been screwing around with her!" She pulled herself free and sat upright.

"Lucinda! What a vulgar thing to say!"

"Is it true or isn't it?"

"Just a little harmless flirting, my love. Just to wear down her resistance a bit."

Lucinda stood up and paced the room. "You're such a liar. Such a goddam liar."

"Lucie, I swear, there's nothing to get upset over. She's far too prissy and proper for anything as complicated as adultery. In fact, I think she has a very happy marriage." He got up and went over to her, held her by her shoulders.

"You seem to regret that," she said testily.

"No, I recognize it and I respect it." He smoothed back her hair with his hand. He kissed her very hard. "*Vieni*, I haven't seen you for almost a week." He drew her toward the bed.

"Stefano, I warn you – if I find out there's been any hanky-panky with this prissy little English muffin… "

He laughed as he pulled her onto the bed and fell on top of her. "'Hanky-panky'! Lucinda, do you realize how old-fashioned you sound?"

"Then I'll say it the most modern way I know. If you've fucked Mrs. Dickson, I promise that the fucking you got from her won't begin to match the fucking you'll get from Contini."

Angrily, she rubbed out her cigarette and wrapped her arms around him.

* * *

As he always did for St.-Cloud dinners, Monsieur Jean had closed off his second dining room and set up one long table to accommodate the guests. His wife, Yolande, made a centerpiece of pink chrysanthemums, folded the starched white napkins her special way, and put three wine glasses at every place: for white wine, red wine, and Champagne. Sybil exclaimed, "How lovely!", and kissed Yolande on the cheek. She shook Jean's hand respectfully, but he was in high spirits, and he raised her hand with an exaggerated gesture and kissed it.

"Madame, you honor us," he crowed.

He led them into the lounge, where some worn but comfortable chairs were scattered about. The fireplace, never used in the summer, was decorated with a large bouquet of gladiolas. Two waiters brought in trays of *kir* and bite-sized pastries filled with crab.

Gérard, Antoine and Vincent went to the kitchen with Jean to look things over, as friends and colleagues.

The evening's menu was to start with *terrine aux écrevisses*, followed by *coq au vin, salade verte* and cheeses, and *soufflé Grand Marnier* for dessert.

Pas mal, pas mal, Gérard said approvingly, inspecting the terrine. On every plate, each slice was decorated with a paper-thin twist of lemon, a bundle of baby green beans, and the pop-eyed head of a crayfish.

Antoine checked the wines. Then he sniffed the *coq au vin* and guessed, correctly, that Jean had prepared it with a good Macon – a Clos de Beaune. "Bravo," he said. And turning to Vincent, "You see, you always must match your products. Burgundy chickens require Burgundy wine."

It was a running argument between father and son: Vincent liked to mix his regions. He shrugged and shook his head. Yolande, a robust woman from Rotterdam, patted Antoine indulgently on the back.

"*Allez,*" she said, "even Jean sometimes mixes things up. If he didn't, we would never have gotten married!"

She hurried into the lounge and announced that dinner was served.

Sybil carefully seated everyone, making sure that Stefano was isolated – far from herself and Mrs. Contini, wedged between Helen Perkins and Mr. Takashi. It was obvious that he didn't like the arrangement. Deftly, he offered his chair to Daniel, saying he had better sit on the other side of the table, with the smokers.

Clever rascal, thought Sybil. He ended up sitting between Lucinda Contini and Patti.

"Smoking really should be outlawed at dinners like these," said Barbara.

"I agree," said Sybil. "As a matter of fact, many great chefs even object to women wearing perfume at dinner."

"I would say a woman's perfume only enhances a meal." It was Stefano, naturally, with a charming nod to the two women flanking him.

"I'd say it would create a terrible conflict in any red-blooded man," said Lucinda, "having to choose between sex and steak."

"Why not both?," smiled Stefano.

"Together?," retorted Lucinda. "At the same time?"

"Time is just an illusion, you know." said Stefano. "The current concept is synchronicity."

"Synchronical sex." Lucinda replied disdainfully, lighting a cigarette. "It sounds dreadful, like mechanical sex."

Sybil didn't understand how the dinner conversation suddenly took such a weird turn. She was determined to change it, but Richard unexpectedly broke in.

"Considering the growing numbers of STD's, almost any kind of sex is problematic these days. Eating is much safer."

Good grief, thought Sybil, here we go. AIDS. Before we even start on the first course. It's getting to be like New York.

"Daniel, would you please pass the bread down the table?"

She tried a diversionary tactic, and it didn't work. Daniel passed the bread, but chimed into the conversation.

"I guess the only sure answer is total abstention," he said. That's not very original, thought Sybil. But she realized that Daniel, infatuated as he was with his work, and often exhausted, could probably give up sex quite easily. In fact, there had been long stretches recently when he did. Could that be a reason for her "lapse" yesterday afternoon?

"Lapse" was the word. It cushioned the memory of that "incident" (another good word). "Lapse" was value-free, it sounded brief and inconsequential. An "incident" of that sort would never happen again.

She stole a glance at Stefano, and was annoyed to see him whispering something in Mrs. Contini's ear. It must have been funny, or was she just flattering him with that loud burst of laughter?

"'We have a friend in Malibu who seems to have AIDS," Patti piped up. Stuart spluttered, just as he was tasting his wine. Dammit, that's not something you brag about, especially in a group like this, and Patti seemed to be beaming with pride.

"Um, he's just an acquaintance, a friend of a friend, really," he said.

"Oh, no – we've known him for years, him and his lover. So far his lover hasn't caught it, but he's awfully worried he will."

Stuart shot her a wilting look, but she chirped on, only aware that everyone was listening to her.

"Actually, we were a little worried, too, because they used to use our hot tub. But our doctor told us it was very unlikely that it spreads that way."

Stuart wanted to disappear under the table.

"That's true," said Richard, "but hot tubs are a potential breeding ground for all kinds of infections. I advise my patients to stay away from them."

Sybil felt ill. She hadn't even thought about the medical risk of her "lapse"; now, on top of guilt and confusion, there was anxiety and alarm. She stared numbly at the orange crayfish on her plate.

"Not that I want to change the subject, but this terrine is wonderful," said Barbara.

Everyone murmured in agreement. Sybil picked up her fork again and dabbled with a puny green bean. Her appetite had vanished.

*   *   *

"It was a great dinner," said Daniel. "Really first-rate."

"Yes," said Sybil wearily. She pulled off her shoes and put them in the armoire, lined up carefully next to the others. She started to unzip her dress, but decided she would undress in the bathroom. Daniel threw his blazer on the chair and said he was going downstairs for a short business meeting. "I'll be back in about an hour."

"All right," Sybil said. She knew Daniel was planning for this as soon as possible after Lucinda Contini's arrival, and she knew she would not be welcome. Right now, she didn't care; she wanted to get to sleep.

Daniel picked up a stack of papers, took a pen from the blazer pocket, and left.

Stefano and Lucinda were already in the salon. Gérard,

Antoine and Vincent were waiting outside, silently. They followed Daniel in.

"Well, let's have a look at it," said Daniel, as they all sat down. He spread his papers on the coffee table. "Gérard, we've talked a bit about the proposal, but maybe we should go over it to make it clear for Antoine."

"Antoine knows as much as I know," Gérard replied. "I've talked to him about it."

Antoine nodded.

"And Vincent knows, too," added Gérard.

Daniel was a little surprised, but he said, "Good. Then let's start right in with questions. What would you like to ask Mrs. Contini?"

Gérard shook his head. "No questions," he said. Antoine shook his head also.

"No questions?," said Daniel. "Does that mean you agree to the sale?"

"It means we don't agree to the sale," Gérard said flatly.

"But we haven't even discussed it!"

"We have discussed it, you and I. And Antoine and I," answered Gérard. Daniel was baffled. He looked at Stefano and Lucinda, who were looking at each other, equally perplexed.

"But Mrs. Contini and Mr. di Carozza are here to answer your questions, and to negotiate. We haven't even discussed price yet."

"No questions, no negotiations. *Merci beaucoup.*" Gérard was intractable, and Antoine obviously supported him. Vincent, though, looked uncomfortable.

"Vincent, do you agree with this?," Daniel asked.

"I would like to hear more about it," Vincent admitted, "but *papa* and *oncle* Gérard say no. So it's no."

Daniel ran his fingers through his hair. This was ridiculous. Was it Sybil's doing?

"Monsieur Bordet," said Stefano, realizing how foolish he and Daniel must look to Lucinda, "the Contini group recognizes that this is a valuable piece of property. They are prepared to pay a great deal for it, and assure you continued participation in its management and development."

Gérard looked at him sternly. "Monsieur, it is not a question of price. And it is not a question of participation."

"Then what is it?," asked Stefano.

"Let us say it is a question of principle, a very old principle."

"You don't want the property to go into foreign hands?," Stefano suggested.

"In a sense, that is correct."

"But this is Europe, modern Europe!," Stefano exclaimed. "In a few years, there will be no barriers, no frontiers, no Frenchmen, no Italians, no Turks. Only Europeans. The whole continent is our country."

"You can change the politics, and you can even change the geography, but you cannot change the history," Gérard said solemnly.

"Gérard," Daniel said, losing patience, "that is a very stubborn and negative attitude, if I may say so."

"Then I am stubborn and negative," he answered.

Daniel and Stefano exchanged looks of exasperation.

Then Lucinda spoke up.

"Monsieur Bordet, I'm an American, so maybe I have a more objective viewpoint in the matter. Personally, I have never understood why Europeans can't cooperate and work together the way we do in the United States. I mean, Europe should be just another melting pot." She took a long draw on her cigarette. "Besides, in today's market, you've got to create big multinational groups in order to compete, to survive. A little wine producer like St.-Cloud isn't going to last very long in this changing world."

Gérard looked at her for a moment, in silence, and then shrugged. "So," he said, "we will starve to death or we will be swallowed up. *Quelle différence*?"

Lucinda could see his mind was set. He was using the kind of argument that she knew the French excel at – a kind of existential I-don't-give-a-damn: *Je m'en fous*. She settled back into the sofa, shot Stefano an icy glance, and gazed up at the ceiling.

Stefano cleared his throat. "Well, it seems we're quite far apart on this. Perhaps we should all just sleep on it for now."

It was clearly the only thing to do. They stood up, shook hands stiffly all around, and headed for the stairs. Antoine and Vincent said a few words to Gérard and then left for the gate-house. Daniel patted Stefano on the shoulder.

"It's not lost yet," he said. "Let's talk to Antoine and Vincent tomorrow."

Stefano nodded, and said goodnight. Then he went over to Lucinda.

"I can't believe it. I had no idea he had made up his mind," he whispered.

"Imbecile," she said. "For this I had to drive to Burgundy?"

At the top of the stairs, she went quickly to her room and locked the door behind her.

*   *   *

Thursday, Sybil knew, was always a drag. It was the midpoint of the course, and the guests were getting tired of the routine, were bloated from the eating and bored with each other. So she always suggested an outing on Thursday afternoon.

"Who would like to take a drive to Beaune today?," she asked at lunchtime. She tried to project some enthusiasm.

"What's at Beaune?," Stuart asked, picking at his salad.

"Well, there's the wonderful 15th century Hotel-Dieu which housed an ancient hospice – that's a hospital – and which has Van der Weyden's famous retable of the Last Judgment, and where the big wine sale takes place every November. And there's the home of the Dukes of Burgundy, which has a special wine museum. And the medieval church of St. Nicolas..." She paused. Was she making any sense? "We can take two or three cars and be there in half an hour."

No response. Then Barbara, bless her, said, "Yes, I think I'd like that. How about it, Richard?"

Richard agreed. Then the Perkins said they would come, and finally Patti and Stuart. The Japanese said no thank you, they had some work to do. Lucinda couldn't make up her mind. "I'd like to get hold of Mr. di Carozza first," she said, "and see what his plans are."

Mr. di Carozza, in fact, had not shown up for the morning class. Lucinda had slept late, knocked on his door around ten o'clock, entered his room, and found no one there. Strangely, his bed had not been slept in.

Where the hell did he sleep last night?, she wondered. Up in the attic with Sybil Dickson? In town with a local damsel? With Stefano, anything was possible. She probably shouldn't have locked him out, she thought, but she had been furious after the meeting. What an utter waste of time to come here!

Sybil wondered, too, where Stefano was hiding; his Ferrari was still parked in the courtyard. Daniel told her before breakfast how badly the meeting had gone, and he blamed her, in an indirect way. He said he was planning to confer with Stefano and Mrs. Contini later in the morning, but much later in the morning, Stefano was still missing.

Too bad, decided Lucinda, I'm not going to waste more time sitting around waiting for him to show up. "I'll go to Beaune, too," she said.

"Good," said Sybil. "That makes eight of us. Daniel, will you come?"

Daniel said no, he had to make some calls to New York.

Sybil quickly assessed the car-passenger ratio, and suggested that Vincent drive Gérard's car with Patti, Stuart and the Perkins and she would take her own car, with the Silvers and Mrs. Contini, and lead the way.

The weather had turned warm again, after the rain. The vines glistened in the yellow haze. Sybil rolled down the window of her Fiat and unconsciously began humming that old Charles Trenet song, *"Douce France"*. For the time being, she had forgotten about Stefano, about 'lapses' and 'incidents'. Nothing seemed to matter but getting to Beaune.

She pointed to an ancient Cistercian abbey off in the distance and started to explain how, in the 11th century, some Benedictine monks decided to leave the opulent Cluny church and set up their own simple community at Citeaux. But her passengers didn't seem very interested, so she kept the story to herself.

Mrs. Contini was sitting beside her in the front seat, rather silent. She asked if Sybil would mind if she lit a cigarette. Sybil said no, of course not, but perhaps she could open her window.

This must be pretty tame to her, Sybil reflected, after dashing around in her Alpha Romeo. She stole a sidelong glance at her. Lucinda had her hair pulled back again, held by a Hermès scarf. She was wearing pale beige slacks, a tailored white silk shirt, masses of gold chains and bracelets, chunky gold earrings, and a mega-carat diamond ring. She had a beige suede jacket over her shoulders. Sybil felt dumpy and drab by comparison, in her sensible skirt and blouse from L. L. Bean, her blue Shetland cardigan, her single gold chain dangling the initial S, and her half-carat diamond engagement ring. She had felt perfectly well turned-out all summer long – why was this woman spoiling it now?

"I think I've read some of your food columns," Lucinda said unexpectedly.

"Oh, have you? How nice."

"I must say, in spite of being in that line of work, you've managed to stay slim."

It was a compliment of sorts, Sybil realized. "You'd be surprised how many food critics do manage to keep their *ligne*. You really don't have to eat a lot to eat well," she replied.

Lucinda inhaled deeply and blew the smoke out the window. "I have a terrible time in Italy. Every meal begins with pasta."

"A dish of pasta alone is alright," said Sybil, "but when it's followed by another course, it's really too much. I've read that Sophia Loren says she eats pasta every day, but I'm sure she has it as a single course."

"Unlike my husband," said Lucinda. "He has a typical Italian appetite, and a typical middle-aged paunch."

"But he's probably eating better than most Americans," said Richard from the rear seat. "No fatty steaks, french fries, ice cream, junk foods."

"True," agreed Lucinda, "but probably a gallon of wine every day, and twenty cups of espresso."

"Any problem with his liver or blood pressure?" Richard's voice had automatically turned professional, Barbara noted, smiling to herself.

"Absolutely," said Lucinda. "He's been under treatment for three months now. But he refuses to change his diet."

"He's going to regret it," said Richard.

"So will I. I'm practically resigned to early widowhood." She sounded, in fact, more resigned than regretful.

"Of course," ventured Richard, still with his professional tone, "you're not doing yourself a favor by smoking."

"Oh, doctor, I know," Lucinda said coyly. "But nobody's perfect. On a scale of one to ten, tobacco is a fairly mild sin."

"It's not a moral question," Richard continued earnestly. "It's a question of your health."

"But that's the problem," said Lucinda, unbuckling her seatbelt so she could turn around to face him. "Americans have turned health into a moral issue. The idea today is that if you're not fit, you're not patriotic. As if you need a sound mind in a sound body to salute the flag."

"Well, I guess it helps," Richard said meekly. Actually, he had never thought of the connection.

"I tell you, I have lived in Europe long enough to appreciate the European mentality. Europeans – Latins, anyway – know that it's not worth living to a hundred if you have to give up the things that make it worth living to a hundred."

Richard was sure he had heard that line in a Woody Allen movie, but he chuckled. He couldn't think of a single remark that would sound half as logical or clever.

Barbara was starting to dislike this woman. She jumped into the dialogue.

"I think it's a question of priorities. At some point, you have to decide whether you go for the quick thrills or the long-term satisfactions."

"Well, I find quick thrills satisfying in the long-term," said Lucinda, "and even for the short-term." And with that, she deliberately lit another cigarette.

"Better buckle your seatbelt, anyway," Richard said amiably. Lucinda shot him a broad smile and snapped on the buckle again.

"I like your bedside manner," she said.

Barbara crossed her arms and looked out the window. She wished there were another man in the car. That Carozza man, for example – what had happened to him? He was an amusing, charming character.

"Where do you suppose Mr. di Carozza is?," she asked. She directed the question to Sybil, but it was Lucinda who answered.

"Stefano? Oh, I imagine he's off on some wild goose chase, as usual."

Sybil was startled to hear her talk about him in such a familiar way.

"Is he like that? I mean, likely to disappear?"

"He tends to be a bit unpredictable," said Lucinda, "which of course is half his charm. But in business he's reliable. He's been working for my husband for a number of years now, and hasn't once let him down."

So, she knows his professional side and his personal side, mused Sybil; I should have guessed. Her hands clutched the steering wheel.

"What *is* your husband's business, if I may ask?," asked Richard.

"He's head of a multinational conglomerate," replied Lucinda, unbuckling her seat belt again. "Contini Enterprises. All sorts of companies – ready-to-wear, light industry, an investment firm, a restaurant chain. His next venture is going to be wine. That's why we're here, looking over St.-Cloud and the other places." She turned to Sybil abruptly. "Exactly why doesn't your chef want to sell?"

Sybil was taken off balance. After Daniel's cat-and-mouse capers, and Stefano's sneaky seduction scene, she wasn't prepared for a woman's direct approach.

"Well, I – um – I think he wants to keep it in the family. He respects tradition, you know. And he feels a massive buy-out in the region would change the entire character of Burgundy. And the quality of its wines."

"He's probably right," Barbara said thoughtfully. "Small is beautiful."

"Small is small," said Lucinda. "Small is inefficient, small is unprofitable, small is totally outmoded in today's world."

"But that's the nature of the wine business," protested Sybil. "That's part of what makes it a luxury product."

"Look," said Lucinda, "I love wine, I love caviar, I love truffles. Why shouldn't these things be produced in larger quantities? Take mink – mink farming gives us more mink, not worse mink."

"Well, as long as you're keeping the quality while you're increasing the quantity, it's alright," said Barbara. "But you certainly wouldn't want to replace diamonds with zircons, or silk with polyester. I mean, they're perfectly suitable substitutions, but you have to admit they're not high-quality, natural products."

Richard was feeling like an outsider in what had become a trilateral women's conversation.

"Listen," he said, "maybe it's not a question of the product at all. Maybe the important consideration is whether it would be good for the region, and the people who live here, to consolidate everything."

"That's an important point, too," agreed Sybil. "These people have their roots here. They know the soil, and the climate, and the plants, and the entire process inside out. Their families go back for generations here. How can you just buy them out, throw them off their land? How can you even recycle them into another business? The French unions scream whenever an auto plant is closed down, or a coal mine is shut, and thousands of workers lose their jobs, but there's absolutely no one around to defend these growers."

"A lot of them could simply stay and go on working here," argued Lucinda. "We'd need their know-how."

"But you just can't produce the same variety and quality if the whole business becomes mass-production," said Sybil, with exasperation.

The discussion had gone full circle. They arrived at the outskirts of Beaune, and she wished she could turn right around and drive back to St.-Cloud.

* * *

It was a pleasure, though, to visit Beaune with people like the Silvers. Barbara raved over the colored tiles on the roof of the Hôtel-Dieu, and was thrilled to see the Van der Weyden.

"It's Art History 105 all over again!," she exclaimed.

Richard, of course, was overwhelmed by the main room of the ancient hospital – a space as big as two ballrooms with built-in beds lined up on either side. Each bed, rather short and narrow, was partitioned off in its own niche, and was hung with heavy curtains.

"People didn't stay here long ," Sybil said. "By the time they finally entered a hospital, you could be sure they were near the end." Being in a grim mood, she relished the grim explanation. "Also, it was very crowded. It wasn't unusual to have two in a bed."

"Leave it to the French, even when they're dying," said Lucinda, loud enough for the next group of tourists to hear.

Patti and Stuart giggled, and Sybil went nonchalantly on.

"You'll notice the pewter pitchers and goblets on each bedstand. They actually did serve wine to the patients, because in those days it was safer to drink than water."

"Still is today, in some places in the world," Richard nodded.

Lucinda smiled at him. "Really, doctor, is that what you recommend to your patients?"

He smiled back. "Only if I want to see them again."

Barbara nudged him and reminded him their camera was in his pocket. "I think your staff at the hospital would enjoy a picture of this," she said. He agreed, and took a flash.

The huge altar at the front of the room, explained Sybil, was not at all out of place, because the hospital was run by a religious order.

"In the end, all you could do was pray," said Lucinda "Honestly, it makes me shudder. It's like those ghastly old hospitals in Italy. 'Abandon hope, all ye who enter here.' That seems to be their motto."

"Well, I suppose a few hundred years from now people will look back at even our best hospitals and say the same thing," said Richard. "Our operating blocks and high-tech equipment are going to look pretty primitive."

"That's not very reassuring," said Lucinda.

Richard shrugged. "We do the best we can with what we've got. The longer you live, the better the treatment you'll get, if that's any comfort to you."

"No, but it's another good reason to live as long as I can."

George and Helen asked to stop and buy some postcards on the way out. Then Sybil suggested taking a break at a café before going on to the wine museum. She sat down next to Vincent and ordered a double expresso.

Ça va?, she asked.

Oui, ça va, he answered. But he didn't sound too happy.

She ventured a question. "What do you think about this proposal to buy St.-Cloud?"

Vincent was silent for a few moments. He didn't look at her when he finally answered. "I think it's a good opportunity. I think my uncle is crazy to turn it down."

"Have you spoken to him? Have you told him that?"

"I told him he should consider it seriously. At first he said yes, he would. But two days later he said he made up his mind. It was no."

"Personally, I think he's made the right decision. And your father seems to agree with him."

"It's nonsense!," Vincent exclaimed. "What do they

know? They're the old generation. They don't understand business. They don't understand that a few years from now Europe is going to be one market, one big federation, and all their beloved bits of land and scraps of property will be insignificant and meaningless."

"But if what you say is so, you'll still be able to sell St.-Cloud later on. It will always be a valuable piece of property, like all the vineyards here."

"No," Vincent insisted. "The time to sell is now. These old people simply have no perspective."

"I can see your point," Sybil conceded, "but I see their point of view, too. They're French, they're Burgundians, and they don't want to sell out their history."

"History belongs in the history books," Vincent said angrily.

"Yes," Sybil agreed, "but they've been through a war. They've lived through a particularly painful segment of history."

"Then it's time they got over it." Vincent ordered another *ballon* of red Burgundy. "Another coffee?," he asked.

"No, thank you," Sybil replied. She wished she could find an answer that would satisfy all of them, and most of all herself. For she realized the heart of the matter was not her sentimentality about St.-Cloud and Gérard and the other growers; really, it involved a basic question about identity – national identity – which requires a shared history, tradition, continuity, pride. But how much? Too much, and you end up with chauvinism, hate, war. On the other hand, she reflected, perhaps the very idea of national identity is obsolete, and we should truly be striving for a higher ideal: cooperation, integration, and unity. And yet, how she hated conformity! How she hated the idea of a homogeneous, anonymous, monotonous brave new world!

Her personal identity was just as confusing, she realized. Was she British?, American?, French? Was she Mrs. Daniel Dickson, or Sybil Dickson, or Sybil Anybody who could have a fling with a suave Italian? She trembled slightly at the memory. Did she still believe in marriage and fidelity, or was she bored with that and ready to explore…. what had Stefano called it?….her sensual side. How could she determine what was best for Burgundy if she couldn't even sort out what was best for herself?

Vincent had fallen silent, too. I must stop thinking of him as a petulant boy, thought Sybil. He's ambitious, that's all, and maybe he sees the future more clearly than I do.

"*Allons*, Vincent," she said, patting his hand, "time to take our guests to the wine museum."

*   *   *

They returned to the château as the sun was starting to slip behind the hills. Sybil could hardly keep her eyes on the road ahead, for a dazzling sunset was frothing in the west: long golden rays shot through pink and orange cloud banks, and the whole sky gradually turned from aquamarine to violet. Her passengers must have been watching it, too – or were they just groggy? – for they hardly said a word all the way back.

She saw Daniel pacing up and down as she turned

into the courtyard. He strode over quickly as she braked to a halt.

"Sybil, this is really crazy. We can't find di Carozza anywhere."

"But his car is here," she said. "He couldn't have gone away."

"That's what's so crazy. He's got to be somewhere in the area. But we've looked all over the grounds, thinking he might have had an accident, and we haven't seen a trace. I even drove into town with Antoine, checked with all the shopkeepers, but no one's seen him."

Lucinda was listening, apparently concerned, and said, "It's not like him to take off like that – not without his car. Are you sure he's not upstairs in one of the rooms?"

Daniel shook his head. "Colette and I have searched everywhere, even in the wine cellar, at the oil press, at the *poulailler*. He has simply disappeared."

"Well, now that everyone's back, let's all take a look," Lucinda suggested sensibly. She knew that even if Stefano had a hangover, which sometimes happened, he'd have pulled himself together by mid-afternoon and resurfaced.

Sybil felt silly calling everyone together and directing them to fan out and search for a missing adult. It was hardly a sophisticated activity, this impromptu game of hide-and-seek. But it had to be done, she sighed. She couldn't wait to see where Stefano would finally be found, and what story he would tell.

The Silvers said they wanted to stretch their legs and offered to walk around the grounds, checking the *dépendances* and the tennis court. Patti and Stuart joined them. The Perkins' were tired, but said they would check all the rooms on their floor, knocking on the doors. Sybil said just knocking wasn't enough, and sent Colette with them with her bundle of keys. Daniel said he'd go, too, and search the top floor again. Sybil herself decided to scour the ground floor and the wine cellar. She imagined finding Stefano in a drunken stupor, with dozens of empty bottles smashed around him. Then she would triumphantly call Lucinda Contini to come and retrieve him.

She scanned the salon first, and then poked her head into her office. Empty. She hurried through the pantry and into the kitchen, where Gérard was decorating *mousses au chocolat* with a squirt of *crème Chantilly*. He looked up only an instant as she entered.

"*Bonjour*. Have a nice trip?"

"Yes, but for God's sake, what has happened to Mr. di Carozza?"

Gérard shrugged. "Who knows?"

"But he can't just have disappeared," Sybil said.

"He's – what do you call it? – a bad penny. He'll turn up again." Gérard calmly put the fourteen little pots in the refrigerator to chill for dinner.

"But it's our responsibility to look after the guests. I mean, that's why we have insurance, in case they have an accident here, or something happens to them."

"But Sybil, if he can't be found, then you can't say something has happened to him, *n'est-ce pas*?"

It was that maddening Cartesian logic. I think, therefore

I am. I don't think, therefore I am not. I am nowhere to be found, therefore I am fine.

"Honestly!," Sybil huffed. "I'm going down to have a look in the wine cellar."

She carefully maneuvered the damp, circular stairs, opened the heavy oak door, and switched on a light. There were no smashed bottles, no Stefano. She walked down the entire row of casks, as if he might be hiding between them, but he wasn't there. So, she reasoned, he didn't drink himself dumb or have a heart attack....at least, not here.

The search was just as fruitless upstairs. Daniel and Colette inspected every room again, even the bathrooms and armoires, and found no sign of him, except in his own room where all his things seemed to be in order – even his wallet, his passport, and his credit cards.

"He couldn't have gotten very far without any of that," Daniel surmised, and Lucinda agreed.

Patti, Stuart and the Silvers returned from their walk and also had nothing to report. Lucinda decided to call up the Contini office in Milan and see if Stefano's secretary had any word from him. But then she realized it was almost seven o'clock, and no one would be there, so she said she would have to wait until the morning. She seemed nervous and annoyed. It was more and more obvious to Sybil that there was something other than business between this woman and Stefano. She wondered what kind of man Signor Contini was, and whether he was aware of his employee's self-appointed perks, but in the end she didn't really care. Her own ego was blistering: she felt very angry and very foolish. She began to hope, in what she knew was a childish reaction, that some divine punishment – not too devastating, of course – had indeed befallen Stefano.

"A penny for your thoughts." It was Daniel, coming up the stairs behind her.

She sighed. "Just wishing this hadn't happened. It's so unnecessary, just diverting everyone's attention."

"Not everyone," he said. "The Perkins' and the Japanese aren't too concerned. The Silvers and the California couple are taking it in a spirit of fun, like some kind of mystery in a haunted castle. It's only you and Mrs. Contini who seem terribly anxious about it." He opened the door to their room.

"And what about you?," Sybil asked.

"I think it's kind of strange. And a bit of a nuisance, too, because I wanted to pursue our talks with Gérard. But I'm sure there's a perfectly reasonable explanation, and he'll tell us all what happened."

Sybil nodded, but she didn't really believe there was anything reasonable about it.

*   *   *

That evening, at dinner, the conversation kept returning to Stefano. It seemed to Sybil that he was even more present in his absence than when he was actually there, being witty and flirtatious.

At first, Lucinda was quiet, nibbling the *coquilles St.- Jacques* and drinking an inordinate amount of Chablis. By the time Gérard served the main course – a *rôti de porc aux pruneaux* – and Antoine uncorked the Gevrey-Chambertin, she had relaxed enough to join in. She was a star witness, in a sense, because she knew Stefano better than anyone else at the table, but even she was at a loss to guess where he might have gone, and why.

"In all the years I've known him, this has never happened," she said. "I mean, he is a little nutty and unpredictable, but he'd never disappear during a business affair ."

"And without his Ferrari," Stuart added. "That's what makes it so hard to understand."

"Sounds like foul play," Barbara said playfully. "It's like a good plot for a detective story."

"I'm afraid we'll have to let the police know by tomorrow if he doesn't show up." It was Daniel. Sybil shot him an anxious look.

"Why?"

"Because he might be lying in a ditch somewhere. He might have had a hit-and-run accident while he was out walking."

"Or a heart attack, or a stroke," added Richard.

"Exactly. In fact, we probably should have notified the police already." Daniel looked worried; he glanced at his watch.

"Let's wait until tomorrow," Lucinda urged. Frankly, she couldn't imagine Stefano taking a midnight stroll along a country road, and as far as his health, she knew he was strong as an ox.

"Well, all right," Daniel agreed. "But if he's not here by the time we finish breakfast, I'm calling the *Commissariat*.

Sybil prayed now for Stefano's quick return. It would be dreadful to have Lucien Dupuis and some of his detectives interfering with tomorrow's schedule, sleuthing around the château and fine-combing the grounds, interrogating the guests.... and me, too, she thought with a start. What could she say? 'Yes, we slept together Tuesday afternoon, but I really don't know him at all. I have no idea where he might be.' Good grief! She looked in panic at Gérard: what would he think of an investigation? He was getting up from his chair and going to the refrigerator to take out the *mousses*. Sybil rose, too, and went over to him.

"Gérard," she whispered, "what do you think? Couldn't we just drive over to the *Commissariat* tomorrow and make a verbal report to Lucien?"

Bien sûr, he said. "But the police will have to come here anyway and investigate. Look through his things, talk to everyone."

"But it will ruin our day. And if anything serious has happened, it will look awful for St.-Cloud. We can't afford to get bad publicity."

"Don't worry," said Gérard. "They'll do what they have to do, and I'm sure everything will work out all right."

She couldn't talk to him any more; he was serving the dessert.

The talk was back to Stefano. Lucinda was feeling giddy now, and picked up on Barbara's joke about foul play.

"That would be incredible," she said. "Can't you see the headlines? – 'Italian Count Bumped off in Burgundy'!"

"'Drowned in Burgundy'!," Barbara laughed.

"How about 'Wined, Dined and Quartered'?" Stuart piped in.

"Or 'Violence in the Vineyards'." That was Lucinda again.

This was really going too far, Sybil thought. "Please," she said, "let's not make any jokes about it. I'm sure he'll be found, and I'm sure everything will be all right." (Hadn't Gérard just said that?) "I'm just terribly sorry that this has disturbed our week together." (No, that wasn't quite what she meant – Stefano had disturbed *her* week.) "Shall we go into the salon for coffee?" (That was the best way out of it all.)

"Lovely dinner," she said to Gérard as she left the kitchen. He nodded solemnly. Antoine was collecting the empty wine bottles, which would be rinsed, as usual, and stored downstairs. Sybil paused a moment in the pantry and asked Colette to bring her a *faux café* – a decaffeinated. She wanted to be sure to sleep tonight.

*   *   *

The telephone rang as she was dozing off. Before she answered it, she looked at the clock – 12:15. Lifting the receiver, she heard the familiar click of a long-distance call.

"Yes?," she mumbled.

An operator was on the line. She had a call for Mr. Cole from Santa Monica.

Oh, God, thought Sybil. "Is it urgent?," she asked "It's from a Mrs. Beck. She says she has to talk to Mr. Cole."

"At this hour!" Sybil corrected herself. It was three in the afternoon on the West Coast. Mrs. Beck had no concept of time zones, or simply didn't care. "Just a minute," she said, and edged out of bed.

"What is it?," Daniel grunted, rolling over.

"A call for Stuart Cole, of all things."

She turned on the bedside light, put on her bathrobe and slippers, and stumbled out the door and down the hall. She knocked on Stuart's door. No answer. Again, harder. Still no answer. Again. Finally, Stuart's voice called out, "Who's there?"

"Sybil Dickson. You have a call from California."

"Jesus."

She heard some scuffling and saw the light come on, under the door. The door opened. Stuart stood there, tying on his robe.

"It's a Mrs. Beck," she said.

"Jesus," he said again.

"You can take it downstairs on the office extension," Sybil said. "I'll hang up in my room."

Stuart thanked her groggily and made his way downstairs.

"Yeah?," he said, picking up the receiver.

"Stuart? I'm sorry to bother you, but...."

"Jeez, it's after midnight." He was in no mood to mince his words. Jenny Beck was a client; he had been handling her divorce for the past year, and from the way things were going, he could see the case dragging on for years to come. Every time they were near a settlement, she or her husband would throw in another proviso. He wondered what had happened now that could warrant an overseas call.

"What's up?," he asked.

"Stuart, you won't believe this. Mike won't let me take my bicycle."

"Your bicycle?" There had been negotiations over a piano, over Baccarat crystal, over stereo equipment and a collection of tapes, but never had anyone mentioned a bicycle. Who worries about a bicycle?

"Jenny, let me get this straight. You're calling me six thousand miles away at midnight for a bicycle?" Jenny was close to sobs.

"Don't you understand, Stuart? This is the weekend I promised I'd go camping with Nick, and we're biking up to the mountains. Mike is just getting revenge on me for dating his best friend, I know it."

Stuart rubbed his eyes and took a deep breath.

"Jenny, where is this bicycle?"

"In our garage. His garage – Mike's."

"And he won't let you take it?"

"No." She sniffled into the phone for emphasis.

"Jenny, what exactly do you expect me to do?"

"Get an injunction so I can get my bicycle."

"Look, Jenny, will you pull yourself together and think straight? There is no way I call the county courthouse in the middle of the afternoon on Thursday and get an injunction for your bicycle before the weekend."

"But we're only leaving on Saturday. There's plenty of time tomorrow."

I can't believe this is happening, thought Stuart. He tried again.

"Yes, Jenny – I can call the judge at his home tonight, tell him it's an emergency, ask him to drop everything tomorrow so he can work on your bicycle, and get you your injunction for Saturday morning. That will cost you a day's fee for the judge, my own fees for about four hours' work, plus charges for long-distance phone calls. You want your bicycle?"

There was silence.

"Jenny, may I make a suggestion?"

She gurgled something in the affirmative.

"Why don't you rent a bicycle? Just for this weekend, you understand. Then, when I'm back, we can work on getting an injunction for you to repossess your bicycle."

There was a long pause.

"Do you really think that's the best thing to do Stuart?"

"Don't you?"

"Yes, I guess so." She was reluctant to give in. "Okay."

Stuart sighed in relief. "Goodnight now, Jenny."

"Goodnight?"

"Jenny, I told you it's after midnight here."

"Oh, gee, I didn't realize it. Did I wake you up?"

"Forget it," he said. "So long."

"Bye," said Jenny.

Stuart hung up and slumped into the chair. How the hell do people get so screwed up?, he wondered. He shook his head. If I'm not careful, he thought, I'm going to end up bonkers, too.

*　　*　　*

CHAPTER SIX - *Les Digestifs*

Friday morning: Stefano still hadn't turned up. Daniel was getting nervous, and even Sybil had to admit it was very queer. Lucinda, most unlike herself, woke up early and came to Sybil's office before breakfast, asking if she could make a call to Milan. She knew the area code, so Sybil left her alone.

Pronto! Sono Signora Contini. Vorrei parlare con Francesca.

Stefano's secretary, Francesca, got on the line. Everything was fine, she said; no, she hadn't heard from Conte di Carozza. No, not a word. Wasn't he in Lacelle? But where had he gone? Lucinda cut short the conversation to avoid any more questions. She only told Francesca to call her immediately if she heard from him.

She went to the pantry for some coffee. Sybil saw from her expression that the call to Milan had been fruitless. Daniel came over to her.

"No luck, huh? Well, I'm calling the police."

Sybil followed him to the office. "Please, Daniel," she said, "don't dramatize it."

"Dramatize? There's nothing to dramatize. It's dramatic enough. Where's the number of the *Commissariat*?"

Sybil handed him the page of emergency numbers. He dialed, and asked for Inspector Dupuis.

Un petit problème, he started to say, but turned the phone over to Sybil. "Here, your French is better." Sybil began to explain that there seemed to be a problem.

"Not 'seem', there is!," exclaimed Daniel.

And that one of their guests was missing.

"Missing?," said Daniel. "He has completely disappeared!"

Has anyone been found in the area?

"Describe him!," insisted Daniel.

Well, could he come over sometime today and look around?

"Not 'sometime' – as soon as possible!" Daniel was growing frantic listening to Sybil's calm, measured French.

That's fine, she was saying. We'll see you after lunch. She hung up.

"After lunch?," Daniel exploded. "That's hours from now!"

"He has to attend a meritorious medal award ceremony this morning at the town hall. Then there's the mayor's lunch, so he'll come over afterwards."

Daniel was exasperated. "Maybe you should have said that someone was axed to death – maybe then at least he'd skip the lunch."

Sybil looked at him, trying to hold her temper. "I did the best I could. And he's doing his best, too."

"But why didn't you tell him it was urgent?"

"Damn it, Daniel, next time *you* get on the phone, and with your fractured French, see if you can do any better."

She stormed out of the office and joined the class in the kitchen.

*　*　*

The morning dragged. Sybil wanted to put off the police visit for as long as possible, but she knew this interminable wait was worse than actually having them arrive. At two-thirty, the dark blue car rolled into the courtyard. Lucien Dupuis and two of his deputies jumped out and walked over to the front door. Sybil was there before them, holding it open.

Bonjour, Inspecteur, she said.

He bowed formally and raised his hand in a friendly salute. It was the one thing Sybil liked about the French police – that courteous greeting. What happened after that was another matter.

She invited them into the salon, where Daniel was pacing back and forth. Lucinda was sitting on the sofa, smoking, and Gérard and Antoine came in from the kitchen. They warmly shook hands with Lucien, and asked if he'd like some coffee or a *digestif.* He said no, thank you – the mayor's lunch had been *copieux.* Besides – he cleared his throat majestically – they were here on business.

"*Alors,* what has happened?" He took out a worn pad and a ball-point pen.

"Well, we don't know," said Sybil. "One of our guests has been missing for the past day…."

"Two days," Daniel corrected her.

"Yes, this is the second day. The last time we saw him was Wednesday night."

"Name? Age? Address?" Lucinda raised her hand.

"Are you his wife?," Lucien asked.

"No, just a friend. He works for my husband."

Lucien looked at her. Suspiciously, Sybil thought. Then he asked for *her* name, age, address. She managed fairly well in French – well enough, it appeared to Sybil, to deduct a few years when she stated her age. When he had all the additional information – the day Count di Carozza had arrived, why he was there, when he was planning to leave – Lucien said he would inspect his room with one of his assistants, and he sent the other detective outside to inspect the Ferrari. Sybil led the way upstairs.

Stefano's room looked immaculate. Colette had tidied it up Thursday morning, not suspecting anything was wrong. The bedspread was slightly rumpled, she said, but it was clear the gentleman hadn't slept there. She hung up his blazer, emptied an ashtray, and left some fresh towels. That was all.

Lucien looked at the clothes in the armoire, opened the bureau drawers, and examined some papers on the desk. He took the passport and the snakeskin wallet with its matching card case. He checked the bathroom – the medicine cabinet, especially, where he found a bottle of aspirin and some mild sleeping tablets. Then he asked Lucinda if he could see her room.

"Of course," she said.

They were gone about twenty minutes, and when they rejoined the others downstairs, Lucien said flatly, "Not much to go on. Very clean. No history of ill health, or business troubles, or personal troubles, or anything of that sort. And no evidence of foul play. So, I'll look around the property now. Maybe there was an accident."

He knew the grounds well, but asked Gérard and Antoine to accompany him anyway. The three men seemed happy to go off alone.

"When I come back, I'd like to talk to all the other guests," Lucien said to Sybil. She nodded dumbly. That was exactly what she had wanted to avoid. Besides, the interrogation would require an interpreter – herself – and take twice as long and appear twice as ominous as any ordinary inquest. She dreaded the prospect.

"What did I tell you?," said Daniel, at her side. "This is serious ."

"Yes, he's doing his normal, serious job," said Sybil, "but that doesn't mean this whole affair isn't a tempest in a teapot. For all we know, Stefano may turn up in the next five minutes." Her voice was angry; she was angry because Daniel seemed to be placing all the responsibility on her, as if she had been negligent somehow.

"I'd like nothing better than for him to turn up," Daniel replied bitingly. "But I'll bet you my last dollar that he doesn't. A man of his culture and intelligence doesn't play tricks like this."

No, thought Sybil; he only plays around with other men's wives. Oddly enough, as Daniel was blaming her anyway for something else, she felt less guilty about her escapade with Stefano. In fact – and she couldn't understand this – she even felt a little smug.

*　*　*

Gérard and Antoine walked on either side of Lucien; his two assistants trailed behind, prodding and prying into every inch of the property.

Dommage, said Lucien to Gérard, "that this happened on your last weekend."

"Yes," Gérard agreed. "It has been a perfect summer up to now."

"This Carozza type," continued Lucien, "what is he like?"

"Smart, chic, an aging Don Juan, so to speak," replied Gérard.

"He came on business, you know – to negotiate to buy St.-Cloud," Antoine added.

"Yes, I know," said Lucien. "Madame Contini told me about that."

"The Japanese want to buy St.-Cloud, too," said Gérard. "Our two Asian guests told me they are here to inspect the place for their company."

Mon Dieu!, exclaimed Lucien. "Are they competing with the Italians?"

"Neither one knows about the other," Gérard replied. "But it's only a matter of time, I suppose, before they both find out."

"So," said Lucien thoughtfully, "you're surrounded by sharks."

"More than you can imagine," said Antoine.

The three men stopped in front of the *poulailler* while the

—168—

two detectives searched inside. They came out shaking their heads and brushing a few white feathers from their jackets.

"Nothing," they announced, and moved on to the olive press.

"Do you think the Asians had anything to do with the Italian's disappearance?," asked Lucien.

"I don't think so," said Gérard. "They get rid of their competition in more subtle ways."

Lucien smiled. "Still, I'll have to speak to them."

They crossed in front of the château and walked over to the stables, passing the well and Antoine's gate-house.

"No use searching there," Lucien joked, "unless you're holding this Italian for ransom."

"He's not worth enough," Antoine replied. "He's not even worth the trouble." He cast a glance at Gérard.

They searched the stables, where the young pickers would be lodged in a month's time. Then Lucien sent the detectives to make a tour of the garden, the tennis court, and the vineyard.

"Well," he said, "I'll talk to your other guests now. Then I'll write up my report and file it with the missing persons bureau in Dijon."

Sybil had assembled everyone in the salon and was waiting anxiously for Lucien's arrival.

"I'm so sorry about this inconvenience," she said. "This is the first time such an odd thing has happened at St.-Cloud. I'm sure it will all be cleared up very quickly."

"It adds a little excitement to our week," said Barbara cheerfully.

"Like a mystery novel," agreed Stuart.

Mr. Takashi and Mr. Okura nodded vigorously. Sybil wondered just how much English they actually understood.

Lucien came in, breathing heavily and wiping his brow.

"That was a nice promenade," he said to Sybil. "Now, do we have a list of all these people?"

"I can draw that up for you," said Sybil.

"Names, addresses and nationality, please," said Lucien.

Sybil went to her office for her ledger. This was really a nuisance. She returned, and sat next to Lucien to help translate his questions. He went from one person to the next, asking about di Carozza and taking notes on his pad.

"He seemed like a friendly sort," George said, "though we didn't talk much to him." Helen agreed.

"He was quite charming," said Barbara.

"A bit of a snob," said Richard. "And argumentative."

"Kind of mysterious," said Stuart. "Like he was hiding his hand."

Lucien looked at Sybil. "Hiding his hand?"

"Like in poker," she explained.

Ah, oui! Lucien turned to Patti. She fiddled with her bracelet.

"Well, he was kind of nice. Old, I mean, but kind of sweet." Stuart looked at her with amazement.

"Are you saying you were attracted to him?" he exclaimed.

"Well, sure. I mean, he was real smooth."

"Smooth?" asked Lucien.

"*Suave*," said Sybil.

Lucien nodded, and scribbled.

The two Japanese managed to explain that they had never spoken to the honorable gentleman, but that he seemed very fine.

"He was a top-notch businessman," said Daniel. "Cultivated, intelligent, highly sophisticated. A pleasure to work with."

"Why are we all using the past tense?," Sybil suddenly asked. "Surely he's still alive."

Peut-etre, said Lucien.

"But this is preposterous," said Sybil. "He's simply disappeared, he's not dead."

"I'll have to notify the Italian consulate in Paris," said Lucien, looking at the deep red passport. He riffed through the pages. He stopped as something caught his eye. "*Tiens!* He was born in Vienna."

"Yes, his parents were Austrian," said Lucinda, who had been standing silently at the window.

"But he has the Italian nationality?," asked Lucien. "And an Italian name?"

"Yes," she said simply. Stefano never liked to talk about his parents, his family. He said he had an Italian uncle who had passed on his name and his title to him.

Un peu bizarre, mused Lucien, looking at the frayed black and white I.D. photo, which must have been at least ten years old. *Oui, un peu bizarre.*

He handed the passport to Gérard, who passed it on to Antoine, who gave it back to Lucien.

"Well, enough questions for today," Lucien announced. "Madame Dickson, *merci beaucoup. Merci à tout le monde.*"

He rose, walked slowly to the door, and signaled Gérard and Antoine to follow him.

* * *

Lucien told his two detectives to wait for him at the car, and he strolled over to the gate-house with Antoine and Gérard.

"Let's go in," he said.

They entered the small parlor which was cluttered with old family photographs and piles of magazines.

"A cognac?," offered Antoine.

Lucien accepted. "I'm partly off duty now," he said, "but only partly." His voice was somber.

The three men raised their glasses to each other without a word. Finally, Lucien smacked his lips and broke the silence.

"Am I crazy, or does this missing Italian remind you of a miserable Austrian?"

Gérard and Antoine stared into their snifters and then gazed at Lucien without a word.

"*Allons, mes amis*, you know what I'm saying. This Carozza character resembles our old friend, Stefan Durschmidt."

Their glances went from one to the other, and Gérard said, "He *is* Stefan Durschmidt."

Lucien put down his glass. He stared out the small curtained window. "What have you done with him?"

There was a long pause. Gérard took another sip of cognac and said, "We went for a walk with him."

"Where?," demanded Lucien. "And when? And where is he now?"

"We invited him to walk around the grounds with us, Wednesday night," said Gérard.

"And what happened? Where is he?"

"He met with an accident," replied Antoine. "He simply disappeared."

Lucien sighed deeply. "You know, you 're placing me in a difficult position. I should search this place right now."

"But you're very welcome to," said Antoine. He poured Lucien some more cognac.

"What do you think you'll find, Lucien?," asked Gérard. "A bloody carving knife? Legs and arms in the freezer? Human tripe in the kettle? Viennese sausage and sauerkraut?"

Lucien ran his hand across his forehead. He looked from one friend to the other.

"You're neither that stupid, nor that bloodthirsty, nor that hungry," he said. "No, I just want to know where the accident occurred, where the body is."

"He fell," Antoine said at last. "He fell fast and far. And he stayed there."

"The well?," exclaimed Lucien.

Antoine and Gérard nodded. And Gérard said, "There's no way to get him out, you know. It's over fifty meters deep.

It's where we dumped all the Nazis' ammunition after they retreated."

"I remember," said Lucien. The three of them, boys, had joined the men, driving around in a farm truck to collect the mortars and shells that were left behind when the German soldiers fled. "And we looked for Stefan, and couldn't find him anywhere."

"We finally realized he must have run off with the Germans," nodded Gérard.

Antoine stroked his glass. "And then it dawned on us that he had been the informer."

"That ambush," said Lucien, "that ambush when they caught your fathers...."

Gérard heaved himself out of the deep armchair, and began to pace the room.

"We were so stupid. We were so stupid. Antoine and I regarded Stefan like any other friend, like any other boy in Lacelle. But he must have heard us talking during school recess about the meeting that night, and he told the German officers."

"We were stupid," agreed Antoine. "We should have been more careful. Stefan was always translating for the Germans, always getting special favors from them, extra rations of coffee for his parents."

"The Durschmidts turned the Bleu Danube into a very comfortable inn for the officers, remember?" Lucien sipped his cognac. "And when the family was finally allowed to go to Switzerland, that winter before the Allied invasion, Stefan pleaded to remain here. So his parents, or the Germans, or someone, found a place for him with the school principal." It was all coming back to him afresh. "But I never understood why he wanted to stay."

"Oh, he had a sense of adventure, I guess," said Antoine. "And he didn't get along well with his father. And I believe, too, he really liked France, after spending all his summers at the Auberge."

"But he also liked the Germans," Gérard added angrily. "He was fascinated by everything that was military."

"True," said Lucien. He fell silent. "So how did you get him to go with you? Did you drag him out of his room?"

"Not at all," said Gérard. "After our business meeting Wednesday evening, which was very short and crisp, Antoine and I went to his room and told him we wanted to talk to him privately. We said we were actually considering the Contini proposal, but wanted to discuss it with him, the direct representative. Not with the American lawyer, and not with the wife of his boss."

"And he agreed? He believed you?" Lucien was surprised.

"People are very foolish and careless, you know, when it's a question of money. Of course he knew who we were, but he was sure we would never recognize him, forty-two years later, with his new name and a new nationality."

"And you walked to the well?"

"Yes," said Antoine. "We talked about St.-Cloud, we talked about Lacelle, and finally, standing by the well – we had pulled the cover off, you see, before dinner – we called him by his name, Stefan Durschmidt. He tried to break away, but we blocked him, and he fell backwards."

Lucien looked at them gravely. "He fell? He wasn't pushed?"

"What difference does that make?," asked Gérard. "The result was the same."

"*Mes chers amis*, we know this is an instance where the ends justify the means, but it is still my job to discover the means."

"Let us say," Gérard said slowly, staring out the window, "that his moving body encountered our unmoving bodies, and he rebounded."

"And you didn't try to grab him?"

"And risk falling into the well ourselves?"

"Besides, it all happened so fast," added Antoine.

Lucien stood up and went to the window. He could see that the well cover had been replaced.

"So," he said, "what are we going to do about our deceased friend?"

"Can't we just leave him where he is," asked Gérard, "on his pile of gunpowder? In any case, it's much too risky to go down there after him."

Lucien had to agree. Even without the ammunition, the well was too old and too deep to explore safely.

"How did you discover his identity?," he queried.

"I heard him humming a German song," said Gérard, "and it rang a bell. The next day, I went to his room with Colette and looked through his papers. His passport gave his place of birth, and his Italian *carte d'identité*, which I've kept, gave his original family name."

"Bravo," Lucien said wryly. "You should have my job."

Gérard smiled at him. "And perhaps you should have mine." He filled the glasses again and automatically the three men raised their hands in a toast.

À la justice, said Lucien solemnly. "Better late than never."

"To the bad old days and to better days ahead," said Antoine.

"To sleeping dogs," said Gérard. "Long may they lie."

* * *

Everyone was jittery Friday night. Gérard, as planned, prepared a light *souper – crudités, quiche Lorraine*, and *poires au vin* – so that the guests could finish early and drive to Dijon for the *Sound and Light* show. Sybil's heart wasn't in it, much as she loved seeing the spectacular lights flashing over the old city hall and the great cathedral. The police investigation that afternoon had thrown a pall over everything, yet now, concerning Stefano, she was more angry than anxious: his unexplained disappearance had practically ruined this last week. And perhaps even more, for if word got around that someone had vanished at St.-Cloud, there was no telling what that might do to next year's registration.

She spoke to Gérard about it while he was preparing supper.

"Don't worry," he said. "This will be kept very quiet. Lucien assures me of that."

"But surely there'll be something in the local paper. And he said he'd have to notify the Italian consulate."

"Just a formality," said Gérard. "The Italians aren't

going to send an investigating team to Lacelle for a missing businessman."

"And the newspapers?"

"Just a small announcement, an *avis de recherche*. This sort of thing happens more often than you think – kids running away from home, middle-aged men leaving their families, cases of amnesia."

"Do you think this is a case of amnesia?," Sybil asked.

"Who knows?," Gérard shrugged. "Maybe he had things to forget."

Sybil watched him lift the poached pears out of the saucepan. He was, as always, imperturbable. There were two classes of Frenchmen, she thought: those who wept (like those Frenchmen weeping in the street when the Germans rolled into Paris, and weeping again when de Gaulle marched victoriously up the Champs-Elysées), and those who don't. Or maybe the French, unlike the Americans, allow crying in public but not in private. The British, she reflected, don't allow it anywhere, while the Italians indulge in it universally, even when they sing.

"Do you ever cry, Gérard?," she asked out of the blue.

He looked up from the pears, amused by the question. "Only at funerals. But not all funerals."

"Public funerals," she suggested.

"Of course," he said.

She smiled. With Gérard, she felt peaceful again. She wished so much that she could erase this past week.

It had exposed so many dreadful things – her shock and anger with Daniel, her discovery of "passion" (mentally, she bracketed the word) with a strange man, her subsequent jealousy (odd, and unjustifiable) toward another woman. She felt off balance, battered; how was she going to pick up her normal life again back in New York? Maybe she needed a few sessions with a shrink, she thought. Her friend Maureen, who had a brief and blistering affair with a 22-year old saxophonist, sought help from a 50-year old Freudian analyst, and ended up having an affair with him, too. "From the frying pan into the fire, from the sax to the sofa," Maureen wailed to her. No, that wasn't for Sybil.

"Why don't you come visit New York this fall?," she asked Gérard. He was spooning the red wine sauce over the pears.

"You're inviting me to Sodom? I'm too old."

"Don't be silly," she laughed. "You're not too old, and it's not Sodom."

"New York is Sodom and Washington is Gomorrah, from what I read these days."

"Oh, Gérard! Are you afraid of bag ladies and beggars?"

"And muggers and dope addicts? Yes."

"Well, it *has* gotten a little worse than when you were there eight years ago," she admitted, "but if you just ignore them, and mind your own business…."

"And pray that they ignore me and mind *their* own business. No, Sybil, *merci*, but I don't think my doctor would approve of such a trip, in any case. He says America is dangerous to one's health."

There was no convincing him. His excuses were flippant, but she knew from his tone of voice that his decision was firm.

"Well, short of hiring a bodyguard for you, and a bullet proof car, I can see I'm not going to lure you over." She dipped her finger into the remaining wine sauce, and nodded her approval.

Daniel came in, agitated.

"Syb, have you seen my tennis racket?"

"Why, it's probably in the umbrella stand, where you always leave it."

"No, it's not."

"Did you look in our room?

"Of course. It's not there."

"Well, I'll have a look when I come up." Sometimes, she thought, Daniel acted as immature as their sons. What is it about marriage that brings out both the bully and the baby in men?

"Please, Syb – I'm packing now."

"But you're not leaving until tomorrow. There's still time to find it."

"And if we don't?"

"Then I'll personally search the place and bring it back with me next week." No, she really didn't want to bother about Daniel's tennis racket next week. So she gave in. "All right, I'll go look for it now." She patted Gérard on the shoulder and went upstairs.

"You've really been in a hell of a mood these past few days," he said to her.

"What do you expect?," she said defensively. "A missing person, a police investigation, and now a missing tennis racket. It's a fine way to end the summer."

"Don't let it out on me. My tennis racket is the least of it."

"The fuss you make over it, it seems to be far from the least."

He sat on the bed and glared at her as she searched the bathroom and the big armoire. There it was, naturally, on the top shelf behind his sweaters. She pulled it out in silent triumph.

"Great," he said, not greatly pleased at all that she had found it in such an obvious place.

"You're welcome," she said sarcastically.

"Thank you," he said sharply.

"Now, unless you need my services to find some other items, I'm going to bathe and change for dinner."

* * *

It was after eleven when the bus lumbered back to St.-Cloud from Dijon. A crescent moon was hanging low over the vineyards, reminding Sybil how infrequently she saw the moon in Manhattan. She glanced across the aisle at the Silvers: Barbara had her head on Richard's shoulder, and he was dozing quietly. They're a nice, happy couple, Sybil thought sadly. She was surprised that the idea of a happy couple made her sad. She looked at Daniel, asleep next to her, hunched against the window, and she knew he was the reason for her sadness. Back in New York, if somehow everything returned to normal, she would like to see the Silvers socially. If everything returned to normal.

Patti and Stuart were sitting behind her, and they seemed to be arguing quietly. Did she hear the word "commitment"? Yes, she did. Oh, Lord, she thought, commitment is only the beginning of it.

Lucinda Contini had begged off the trip to Dijon. She had called the Milan office again, had spoken to her husband, and even rang up Stefano's apartment, telling the maid to call back if she had any word from *signore il Conte*. Her immediate problem, in view of Saturday's departure, was how to get Stefano's Ferrari back to Milan. Finally, she had the bright idea to ask Vincent if he'd like to drive it down. He was stupefied, and quickly said yes.

"We'll pay your fare back, of course," she told him, "but why don't you plan to stay in Milan a few days and meet the Contini group?" Whatever had happened to Stefano – the bumbling, irresponsible bastard – she wasn't ready to give up the Burgundy campaign.

* * *

CHAPTER SEVEN – *L'Addition*

The farewell lunch on Saturday was always a surprise menu. There was no morning class, in order to give everyone time to pack and take a last stroll. As most of the guests would be returning by train to Paris, Sybil arranged for Claude to come with the mini-bus and drive them to the station in Dijon. Usually, there was an hour or so free before their TGV left, so they had time to visit the Beaux-Arts Museum and buy a pot of Dijon mustard.

Barbara and Richard had kept their rented car, and were looking over roadmaps when Sybil came downstairs. They asked her what would be the most scenic route back to Paris, and without hesitation she advised them to follow the Saone River north from Seurre to Talmay, then follow the barge canal up to Chaumont, and from there head west to Paris.

"It will take longer than the autoroute," she said, "but you'll see some wonderful scenery."

They marked it out on the Michelin map.

"You know," said Barbara, "we really must get together when we're back in New York. I think we're practically neighbors."

"Yes, that's true," said Sybil. "I'd like that very much." She went to her office and came back with a visiting card. "You must come to dinner one evening, though I can't promise you anything like Gérard's cuisine."

"I'm sure by now you're his star pupil," smiled Barbara.

Daniel came to the door and asked Sybil if he could see her for a moment. She excused herself. He sounded upset.

"Sybil, did you know these two Japanese guys are after St.-Cloud?"

"What do you mean, Daniel, 'after St.-Cloud'?"

"Just what I said – they represent a big Japanese conglomerate that wants to buy into Burgundy vineyards!"

"Well, that sounds familiar, doesn't it?" She was startled, but amused. Daniel could see neither the irony nor the humor of the situation.

"For God's sake, Sybil, they've been talking to Gérard and Antoine!"

"Not with any success, I imagine."

"I don't know," Daniel sighed. "But do you realize what this means? Contini will be bidding against big bucks."

"Big yen," she corrected him.

He looked at her, exasperated. "I can't believe you're on their side."

"I'm on no one's side," she said. "And frankly, I don't think anyone's going to buy St.-Cloud. Gérard seems dead set against selling."

"Then we're all back to square one," Daniel said. He shoved his hands into his pockets and gazed at her.

"Maybe we are," she answered. And in more ways than one, she thought to herself.

At lunch, she made a toast to Gérard and to a safe trip home for all her guests. Barbara and Richard exclaimed *Vive la France!*, and Gérard cordially answered *Vive l'Amérique!*

Lucinda was sitting next to Vincent, discussing the drive to Milan. Sybil heard her say something about taking a break for dinner in Como.

Gérard prepared a mouth-watering *chaud-froid* for dessert: a combination of cold peach *granité* with a warm custard sauce. Then, over coffee, Sybil handed out the diplomas. She had carefully hand-lettered the names on each one.

"I don't promise this will get you a job in a three-star restaurant," she joked, "but you can hang it in your kitchen and impress your friends."

By three-thirty, everyone was gone. She felt a certain let-down, as she always did at the end of a season, but also a certain relief. Daniel said he'd ring her from the hotel that evening; he'd be staying at the airport in order to make his early flight the next morning. The Perkins' were flying back to Dallas, Patti and Stuart to L.A., and the Japanese to Tokyo. The Silvers were staying on a few more days in Paris. Sybil wondered where she would go, if given a choice; grimly, she thought she could use a few years at a monastery in Tibet.

"That's nonsense, Sybil," Gérard guffawed when she mentioned it to him that evening, half in earnest, as they sat together on the terrace. "That's an intellectual luxury and a waste of time."

"No, it would be a kind of vacation. A chance to clear my head and recharge my batteries."

"Your head and your batteries are perfectly fine," he said.

"I don't know. So much has happened this past week.

I mean, those vultures from Italy and Japan. And Daniel's involvement with them. And Carozza's disappearance, still unexplained." She stopped there. She certainly wasn't going to discuss her "lapse".

"Well," sighed Gérard, "maybe I'm not as sensitive as you. But I think the week went well. A number of issues were laid to rest." He sipped his expresso peacefully.

What issues did he mean, besides his decision not to sell St.-Cloud? Perhaps he had re-examined his will, and set specific terms for Vincent's inheritance. Sybil decided not to question him about it.

"Tomorrow," she said, "we can start going over the books."

Gérard nodded.

"And take a look at the calendar to decide on next year's schedule."

He nodded again. "You see? You're not thinking about your monastery anymore, or any of that religious nonsense."

It was true. Her head and battery problem was getting sorted out, just sitting here sipping coffee. Sipping coffee, she thought, was probably the Western equivalent of meditation.

Sybil studied the last dregs in her cup, as if they were tea leaves. "I know," she said slowly, "I know you're not a religious person."

"I'm not," Gérard answered. "But I believe in miracles."

"You believe in miracles?" Sybil stared at him in disbelief.

"Of course. A miracle is only a natural occurrence that we can't explain. The unfortunate thing is, as soon as we find an explanation, we stop calling it a miracle. But it still is."

"What, for example?"

"For example, wine. A miraculous transformation of sugar into alcohol. Or – a miraculous fusion of flour and butter that produces a pastry." He paused, as if he had already said too much. But he went on. "You know, sometimes I understand what those alchemists were doing. I sometimes think that what they were doing in a crucible, I'm doing – on a different level, of course – in a saucepan."

Sybil looked at him in wonderment. For an instant, she thought she would say something funny, because it *was* funny in a way, but then she saw the grave expression on his face. She swallowed her words.

"I've never heard you talk like this, Gérard. I never knew you thought these things."

He shrugged; he seemed a little embarrassed. "Maybe I was never aware of them – how do you say? – consciously. But sometimes you need a terrible shock to make you aware."

"But have you had a terrible shock?" She was leaning forward in her seat. Gérard, though, turned his head and looked away.

"Gérard, excuse me. But is there something I should know? Or is there something you can't tell me?"

He looked at her now. "This Carozza – he brought back a lot of memories to me."

"But how?"

"Don't ask me how. But believe me, his presence here

was like a dream, or a nightmare. Or a kind of miracle."

"His presence disturbed me, too," admitted Sybil, venturing into deep water.

"He was an attractive man. I'm sure you noticed that."

Sybil was silent.

Gérard continued cautiously. "Of course, husbands never notice these things. And especially not Daniel, who saw him only as a business partner."

Sybil stared at him, troubled and tense. She didn't dare say a word.

"What I want to assure you, Sybil, is my absolute loyalty to you. Because I know you've been worried about your scarf."

"My scarf? What do you mean?"

"The scarf you left in his room. I've disposed of it."

Her mind reeled backwards, in a panic. My God!, the Liberty scarf she'd been wearing. She had left it behind, she had forgotten all about it. She looked in terror at Gérard.

"It's all right, Sybil. I disposed of it."

"What did you do?," she stammered. "I never even realized…." She stopped, catching her breath. "Gérard, how did you find it?"

"Wednesday morning, when I inspected his room with Colette."

"But why did you go to his room? And why didn't you give me back the scarf?"

Gérard could see that she was too nervous to think clearly.

"Sybil, first of all, I didn't want anyone to know I had

been to his room. Secondly, I didn't know why your scarf was there and I didn't want to make you uncomfortable about it. Thirdly, once Carozza disappeared, I certainly didn't want your scarf involved. So I got rid of it."

"Where?"

"Along with Carozza."

She looked at him incredulously. "You got rid of Carozza?"

Now it was Gérard who had to tread carefully. "There was a debt to be paid, something long overdue. Something from the war. The man was an impostor, a criminal. Please, Sybil, we won't talk about it anymore. We are not confessing to each other. We are only affirming our friendship."

Sybil was numb – numb with confusion, numb with dread. Stefano, with his strange accent and his musky scent, was looming over them. He had come from an unfathomable place to intrude on their lives. For Gérard, the intrusion seemed to bring a wave of peace and serenity; for her, it brought a gust of doubt and disorder. And she understood, too, from what Gérard was saying, that she would never see Stefano again. Even if one day she should look back and laugh at the entire episode, Stefano would not be there to laugh with her.

"Are we friends or conspirators?," she asked, quietly.

"Friends, of course; not conspirators," Gérard replied. "My story is all mine and your story is all yours."

But your story seems to be over, and mine is still nagging at me, she thought. No, let's not dramatize this thing. She poured more coffee into their cups and watched the sky darken.

Stefano, with his arrogance and charm, his jokes and his lies, was not unlike Daniel, really. The idea startled her. Even lovely Barbara and silly Patti, even serious Richard and cocky Stuart, even the Perkins' and the Japanese, were mirrors of each other, just plucked and packaged differently. And even this vineyard, this château, and her apartment in New York and her house in the Hamptons, were facets of her life, not to be compared but deeply cherished.

She reached out and put her hand on Gérard's arm. He looked like a man who had come to terms with something – with life? She wondered if she would look that serene in twenty years. She wondered what surprises and turmoil and joy lay ahead. She thought Gérard must be wiser than she ever imagined, and she wanted to ask him a hundred questions. Instead, she just said, "Gérard, in the end, what's the most important thing to you in life?"

Surprised, he looked at her, then gazed into his cup. "Perfection, I think."

"But perfection doesn't exist!"

He smiled. "That's why it's important."

*   *   *

* * * * *

Red Burgundy
© 2012 Second edition
Joan Z. Shore
GG/F Press, Paris, France

www.ingramcontent.com/pod-product-compliance
Lightning Source LLC
Chambersburg PA
CBHW072132170626

46813CB00004BA/1536